CHEERLEADERS®

#20

STARTING OVER

PATRICIA AKS AND LISA NORBY

SCHOLASTIC INC.
New York Toronto London Auckland Sydney

ISBN 0-590-40190-4

Copyright © 1986 by Patricia Aks and Lisa Norby. All rights reserved. Published by Scholastic Inc.

12 11 10 9 8 7 6 5 4 3 2 1   8   6 7 8 9/8 0 1/9

CHEERLEADERS®

STARTING OVER

CHEERLEADERS

Trying Out
Getting Even
Rumors
Feuding
All the Way
Splitting
Flirting
Forgetting
Playing Games
Betrayed
Cheating
Staying Together
Hurting
Living It Up
Waiting
In Love
Taking Risks
Looking Good
Making It
Starting Over

CHAPTER 1

Olivia had been relaxing in a hot tub for ten minutes, musing about the weekend she'd spent at the cheerleading clinic. There was so much to think about, to sort out in her mind. And since she did her best thinking in the bath, she could have stayed there much longer if her mother's booming voice hadn't disturbed her.

"Aren't you ever getting out of there?" Mrs. Evans shouted from the kitchen of their ranch house. "Too much soaking will make you weak. Besides, supper will be ready soon."

Olivia answered through gritted teeth, with as much civility as she could muster, "I was just getting out, Mother."

Olivia had had too many major battles with her mother, an unreasonable, domineering woman, to make an issue over something as insignificant as taking a bath. When she was very little, Olivia's heart problems had necessitated surgery. Although she had made a complete and rapid recovery, her mother was overprotective to an extreme degree. A sniffle, according to Mrs. Evans, might mean pneumonia; rosy cheeks in the winter were a sign of frostbite; and an ordinary stomachache was a symptom of appendicitis.

The fact was, Olivia *did* look fragile. Her slight, graceful build and deep brown eyes gave her a doelike appearance which belied a strong body. She was the smallest but one of the most agile of the Varsity Cheerleaders, and unquestionably the finest gymnast on the squad. And although her mother was a large-boned, heavyset woman whose mere presence was overbearing, Olivia was not afraid to stand up to her. Trying out for the squad against her mother's wishes was a hard-fought battle . . . just one of many that Olivia had had to endure.

Olivia quickly toweled herself dry, slipped into a clean pair of jeans and a Tarenton High T-shirt, and hurried into the dining area to set the table. The weekend had been emotionally trying, and Olivia wasn't up to coping with her mother's warnings and reprimands. She figured she'd ward them off by doing the household chores that were expected of her, have supper, clear away the dishes, and go to her room. There hadn't been time all weekend for homework, and she had plenty of it to do. Of course, if she mentioned that, her mother would immediately say, "I told you not to waste your time at the clinic. Now you're going to be up half the night when you need your sleep."

Olivia sighed, just thinking of the imaginary

conversation, and wondered wistfully what it would be like to have a parent she could talk to. Her father was a quiet, mild man who wanted peace at any price. Although Olivia knew he was on her side, it was only on rare occasions that he voiced an opinion that contradicted his wife's.

Olivia carefully placed the silverware beside the place mats, and thought about Walt Manners, her first real romance. Walt was one of the two male members of the squad, and totally different from Olivia in personality and background. Unlike Olivia, who was quite serious, he was easy-going and liked to clown around. His mother and father ran the local TV morning talk show. It was filmed in their unusual house, a combination of rustic logs and sleek glass, located in the woods.

Walt grew up surrounded by minor celebrities — and some not so minor. Nationally known authors, rock stars, and Hollywood types were featured on the show, as well as local residents. Walt had adjusted at a very early age to having his house filled with strangers — the camera crew and technicians were there daily, along with the special guests, and Walt had become accustomed to their presence.

"Olivia, you must be finished by now. Would you please mix the salad and bring it in while I get your father away from the TV? I want to sit down before this stew gets cold."

"Okay," Olivia said, and went into the kitchen. She figured if she played the part of dutiful daughter, the meal would be bearable.

When Olivia and her father had seated themselves, Mrs. Evans brought in the meal and stood at the head of the table. She looked more like an army sergeant than ever as she portioned out the stew. Then she served herself and settled in her chair.

"I'm certainly glad the cheerleading season is over — no more football and basketball games, and thank heavens they don't need you for baseball. All this leaping around is much too strenuous for a girl with your medical history."

"Mother, I was fine all year."

"You were just plain lucky. And I repeat, I'm *glad* it's over."

"Not quite. You know we have to prepare for Field Day. That's probably the most exciting event of all."

"What are you talking about?" Olivia's mother looked stricken, as though her daughter had announced that she planned to go over Niagara Falls in a barrel.

"You know what it is." Olivia tried to keep the impatience out of her voice. "The last Saturday in May, right before graduation, we have all these athletic events: relay races, broad jumps and high jumps, hundred-yard dash, gymnastics. . . ."

"What's this got to do with you and cheerleading?"

"After everyone else has done their thing, the marching band plays and the cheerleaders perform. At the very end, the old Varsity Squad hands over its pompons and megaphones to the new one."

"Sounds ridiculous. With all the work you have to do the last month of school, I'd think the ad-

4

ministration would have a little more sense than adding extra activities to your schedule. Maybe you could be excused."

"No way. This is fun, and I'm going to do it no matter what you say, Mother."

"What do you say, Norman?" Mrs. Evans asked her husband. "Don't you think this is just too much for Olivia?"

"I think Olivia's done well all year, and if she wants to take part in — "

"Oh, you two." Olivia's mother sighed. "I don't know why I bother to say anything. At least I won't have to worry about all this next year."

Olivia was tempted to say, Don't be too sure. She was only a junior, but since she wasn't absolutely sure herself whether she wanted to try out for next year's squad, she decided to keep quiet.

"I'm thinking of putting in some new rose bushes," Olivia's father said, tactfully changing the subject.

"I don't know why you bother," his wife grumbled. "The Japanese beetles destroyed the old ones."

"There's a new spray that's supposed to take care of that. . . ."

"What makes you think it'll work?"

Olivia tuned out the argument about rose bushes, grateful that she was no longer the subject of discussion. After the dessert of vanilla pudding, she quickly cleared away the dishes, stacked them in the dishwasher, and escaped to her room.

Then she settled down at her desk, pulled out her math book, and attacked her assignment.

Math was Olivia's best subject, and she thought it would be a good way to get started on her homework. But she was only in the middle of the third algebra problem when her mind started wandering.

Her mother's opinions invariably had a negative effect on Olivia, but tonight they reinforced a nagging doubt about whether she really *did* want to be a Varsity Cheerleader next year. Health had nothing to do with it, even though the hard training often made her tired. That was the least of it. There were a hundred other factors that made her think twice about rejoining the squad. She would have to try out again, an agonizing ordeal since the new competition looked very tough, and their dynamic coach, Ardith Engborg, would bend over backward to not show her any favoritism. Also, all the members of the old squad would be graduating and she would have to adjust to five new personalities.

On the other hand, she thought there was nothing as exhilarating as executing a complicated routine with the squad, each member dependent on the five others, and getting wonderful results. Because of her size, as well as her exceptional abilities, Olivia was the gymnastic star. She was the one who was at the top of the pyramid, or executing a backward twist and flip that would make the audience gasp with astonishment. Even if she made the new team, she might not hold this privileged position. There were some new kids planning to try out who looked just as good as she did . . . maybe better.

If she was absolutely honest, she had to admit

that Jessica Bennett, a new candidate with dark hair, sparkling green eyes, and a lithe, graceful body, was every bit as qualified a gymnast as she. Besides, she was a fresh face and maybe the judges would subconsciously find that a favorable factor.

Olivia had never been jealous of the three other Varsity girls, mainly because they all respected her spectacular prowess, but also because they recognized that she and Walt were a couple. Mary Ellen Kirkwood, the captain of the squad, was the girl most likely to invite jealousy, but Olivia never thought of her as competition. Mary Ellen was exceptionally beautiful — a slender, honey-blonde with blue eyes—but because money had always been tight in her home, she was more interested in having a rich boyfriend, or a glamorous career in modeling, than anything else.

Olivia knew that Mary Ellen suffered because she had so little money. Mary Ellen desperately wanted to escape her background, but she had trouble reconciling her ambitions with the indisputable truth that she loved Patrick Henley, a muscular six-footer with a good sense of humor, who unfortunately was a garbage man. After school and on weekends, Patrick actually drove his own truck and collected trash. Getting involved with a garbage man was not part of Mary Ellen's game plan. Then there was his growing moving business — more menial labor, as far as Mary Ellen was concerned.

Olivia had always gotten along with Mary Ellen, and they enjoyed a mutual respect. It had never occurred to Olivia to envy her.

Olivia chewed on the end of her pencil and thought about the two other girls on the team. She'd never been the least bit jealous of them, either. Nancy Goldstein was also sensational-looking, but totally different from Mary Ellen. She had thick, dark hair, a tawny complexion, and a beautiful figure. She was always involved with a guy, most recently Eric Campbell, a quiet, good-looking, determined young man who was training to be a physical therapist. Nancy was an excellent cheerleader, but not in Olivia's class as a gymnast. Olivia had always been friendly with Nancy, but she'd never thought of her as a competitor — on the cheerleading team or in life.

Olivia, like everyone else, thought Angie Poletti was in some ways the soul of the squad. She was warm and caring, and her radiant smile could melt the coldest heart. She was the kindest, friendliest girl in the world, and everyone loved her. Without ever being cloying or overly senti-mental, Angie had a genuine desire to see that her friends, like her, were happy.

Olivia shook her head, as if she could rid her-self of the jealous feelings that loomed over her for the first time in her life. She puzzled over why the fantastic-looking Mary Ellen and Nancy, and the much-loved Angie, had never made her the least bit jealous. Why should Jessica Bennett, whom she hardly knew, and who seemed nice enough, make her so uneasy? Jessica hadn't said or done anything unkind to her or anyone else. She certainly wasn't like Vanessa Barlow, whose father was the superintendent of schools, and who behaved like a queen. Vanessa, because she hadn't made the squad, had made her sole purpose in life causing trouble for the cheerleaders.

Olivia got up from her desk, went into her bathroom, and splashed cold water on her face. It was a trick she used to get herself to stop thinking about something. "I'll be up all night," she muttered, "if I don't stop dwelling on this." Then she blotted her face dry and reminded herself of something Walt had once told her: "Sometimes problems solve themselves if you just wait long enough."

CHAPTER

Ardith stood in the center of the gym and blew her whistle three times. The thirty or more students, wearing shorts, leotards, or warm-up suits, who had been talking animatedly about pikes, pyramids, and split jumps — an outsider might have thought they were speaking a foreign language — immediately quieted down. They all knew Ardith was a tough taskmaster, and especially demanding of the cheerleaders. It wouldn't have been an exaggeration to say that her goal was perfection for the squad. As a result, Tarenton High's cheerleaders were renowned throughout the region for their excellence.

Their work was unusual, with twirling and swirling and pompon-waving. But the Varsity Squad went far beyond the standard routines. They performed dazzling gymnastic feats, elaborate stunts that required each member of the squad to be in top physical and mental condition.

Ardith had single-handedly changed the image of cheerleading. It was no longer a tame extra-curricular diversion, but a challenging and dynamic sport.

Preston Tilford, the only boy on the team besides Walt, had totally revised his first impression of what cheerleading was about. When he saw Walt practicing a stag jump — even the name appealed to him — and tried it himself, he knew for sure that the maneuvers weren't for wimps.

Pres was also aware of the side benefits of being a cheerleader: He worked closely with four terrific girls on Varsity. Pres was one of the most attractive boys at Tarenton — he was well-built, had dark blond hair, and was loaded with sex appeal. He also happened to be from a rich family and had his own red Porsche. Although it was easy for Pres to attract girls, he never took advantage of them. Still, he loved the fun of working out with some of the most appealing girls in the school.

Cheerleading was just one of many differences Pres had with his parents. A more serious problem was their disagreement about his future. The Tilfords were formal, stuffy people, and Pres deeply resented his father's assumption that he would go into the family business, Tarenton Fabricators. They had an ongoing war about the younger Preston's future plans, and neither of them wanted to give an inch.

"Welcome, everyone," Ardith said. "I'm glad to see so many potential cheerleaders." She beamed at the students who were scattered around the gym. "As you know, tryouts are the last week in May, which doesn't give us too much time. However, if you train regularly, there's no reason why you won't be prepared. All I ask is that you do your best. Then, even if you don't make the squad, you will have the satisfaction of knowing you tried your hardest."

"I can't wait to get started," a girl with a silvery voice cried out. It seemed to be an involuntary outburst, and everyone turned to see who had expressed what many of them were feeling.

"I love your enthusiasm, Tara, and I think I'm getting the message: Less talk and more action," Ardith said smiling.

Tara responded with a light ripple of laughter that made her dark eyes sparkle. She was an extraordinary-looking, slim redhead with a flawless complexion — no freckles for her.

"By the way," Ardith added, "this is Tara Armstrong. It would take too much time to tell you everyone's name, but I hope you'll all introduce yourselves to one another. The present squad, I'm sure, will do everything they can to help you — show you the maneuvers that you're having trouble with, teach you the cheers, whatever you want. The old Varsity members will act as mentors, or guiding lights, to the new candidates. I know they want to maintain the reputation of Tarenton's cheerleaders, and their help is essential."

"Right on!" Angie shouted, and the crowd cheered appreciatively.

"Let's do some warm-ups first — stretching exercises, sit-ups, and toe-touches," Ardith continued. "Then I'd like to see the new candidates leap across the gym one at a time. One of the important things you must learn is to enjoy having an audience. If you're too self-conscious, you'll never make it as a cheerleader."

"And don't forget to smile, even if it hurts," Walt said, making everyone laugh.

"Mary Ellen, will you start the exercises?" Ardith asked.

"Sure," Mary Ellen answered, and moved confidently to the center of the gym.

For the next fifteen minutes she led the group in a series of calisthenics. Then Ardith asked the Varsity team to demonstrate consecutive leaps, beginning at one corner and bounding diagonally across the floor to the other end of the gym. Mary Ellen started off, followed by Pres, Angie, Nancy, Walt, and Olivia. Their efforts were impressive, and obviously appreciated by the others, who applauded enthusiastically.

"Thank you for that excellent example," Ardith said as the Varsity members scattered to the bleachers. "Now, let's have everyone else take a turn. Please tell us your name before you begin. Now, who will lead off?'"

The candidates had crowded together in one corner, as if for protection. They all looked a little ill at ease, except for one petite, sharp-featured, short-haired brunette, who pushed herself ahead of the others.

"I'll start," she volunteered. "My name is Holly Hudson." She raised her head and arched her back as though she were about to take a running dive off a high board. Everyone recognized Holly, who was known throughout the school for her modern dancing. She had performed her own unusual work at a school dance recital at Christmas time. So it wasn't surprising that she was completely at ease as she leaped lithely across the floor. The others followed, one at a time, with varying degrees of success.

Olivia had gravitated to Walt's side in the third row of the bleachers, and the two of them commented on each person's performance. They couldn't help but be a little patronizing, since they were so experienced.

"I'd give Holly a seven or eight on a scale of one to ten," Walt said.

"Me, too," Olivia agreed. "A little too much of a show-off."

They watched half a dozen others, and shrugged their shoulders, rating them fives and sixes. Then Peter Rayman, a sandy-haired, slim, but strongly built boy crossed the floor in brisk, clean leaps that made Olivia remark, "He's good! Really good!"

"You're right, Livvy. Amazing how this one exercise reveals so much," Walt said.

"Bet anything he'll be chosen for the Varsity."

"Probably, but it's hard to believe I can be replaced. Maybe you'll be standing on his shoulders next year instead of mine."

"Maybe," Olivia murmured, "if I make the squad."

"You've got to be kidding, Olivia. Of course you'll make the squad."

"Not if I don't try out."

"Of course you're going to try out!" Walt

frowned at the absurdity of what she was saying and turned his attention to the next performer. "Hey, look at this one. That's Carla Simpson — I can't believe she'd even bother to come here."

Carla was overweight, but amazingly agile.

"She's not bad," Olivia commented. "If she were ten pounds lighter she might have a chance."

"You're right. She's not bad at all, but she just doesn't look the part."

"Look who's coming up next — Samantha Gray."

"What a beauty!" Walt exclaimed.

Samantha, a tall, willowy blonde with classic features, was considered the heartbreaker of Tarenton High. She never actually led boys on; she just looked at them and they fell for her.

"It's not just looks we're judged on, remember?" Olivia reminded him.

"I know, I know. But look, she moves well, too."

"Fair," Olivia said, laughing. "But not nearly as well as Peter Rayman."

"You win," Walt said. "Besides, she's not my type. I like smaller women . . . they make me feel strong." He put his arm around Olivia and gave her a quick hug.

Five more boys tried out, but Olivia and Walt decided that the only ones who came close to Ardith's standards were Sean Dubrow who had been at the clinic, and Rob Reynolds who had never come out for any sport. Sean, a lifeguard type, was movie-star handsome, and had an electric smile. He rivaled Pres in looks, but unlike Pres, he wasn't interested in anyone but himself.

The fact that he was a superb athlete added to his charisma.

Rob was much less impressive-looking, but he had a neat, muscular build. He was too short for basketball, and too small for football, so cheerleading suited him perfectly. He executed the leaps nicely, but with deadly seriousness.

The rest of the girls took their turns, and Olivia and Walt continued to evaluate them. They decided that Hope Chang, with her straight, coalblack hair, gentle eyes, and shy smile, had a very good chance. Her leaps were precise and disciplined, as though she had done them all her life.

Tara Armstrong was outstanding — as much for her remarkable looks as for her agility. Her red hair fanned out behind her as she flew across the gym like a comet.

Then Jessica Bennett said her name and started. Her performance was electrifying, and elicited spontaneous remarks from several candidates who, minutes before, were obviously getting impatient to go on to something else. "Look at her go!" "Wow!" "She's too much!"

"She must have been practicing with Mary Lou Retton," Walt said.

Olivia could feel the knot in her stomach tightening, and felt her face get warm. It was true, Jessica was fantastic, and every competitor knew it. She was the only candidate who was applauded when she finished crossing the gym.

Olivia knew she had to say something, and hoped her voice wouldn't crack. "She's a gymnast, you know, so naturally she'd be good." The minute the words were out of her mouth, she wished she could take them back.

Walt gave her a funny look, and said, "There are plenty of gymnasts here, but they don't move like that! Jessica's definitely a ten!"

Olivia nodded her head, not wanting to risk saying the wrong thing again. Instead, she pretended to be very interested in the last two girls who performed: Sally Cook and Betsey Dodson.

"They're quite good," she remarked, faking enthusiasm.

"Medium," Walt said. "But Jessica's such a tough act to follow, they're at a disadvantage. Nobody could look good after her."

Once again Olivia froze, unable to speak. Even though she knew he was right, she wasn't about to agree with Walt. That would only reinforce his view of Jessica. And if she said anything negative, her jealousy would be obvious.

She was spared for the moment by Ardith's next announcement. "I'd like the rest of the time this afternoon to be an informal period where the newcomers will mix with the squad. Don't hesitate to ask for help. You might break up into groups of five or six, with one Varsity member coaching you."

"You mean spread the wealth," Pres said.

"Exactly," Ardith chuckled. "And I'll be here to answer any questions."

As soon as Ardith finished speaking, Pres and the other, senior members of the squad rose, and scattered around the gym. The candidates trotted over to them, and soon the place was alive with movement. The squad members proudly demonstrated the maneuvers that were requested, and then coached the novices who tried to imitate them. They did tumbles and flips, somersaults and cartwheels, twirls and splits.

Olivia was the only Varsity cheerleader who hadn't budged. She knew sooner or later she'd have to participate, but for the moment she hoped to be an invisible observer. Naturally her eyes were drawn to Walt.

To her dismay, she saw that Jessica was in his group. Was that Walt's doing or Jessica's, or had it just happened? Whatever the answer, it was clear that they were talking together. The next thing she saw was that Walt had clasped his hands around Jessica's waist and was lifting her onto his shoulder.

Olivia seethed inside, not knowing whether she was more apt to cry or kill. She took deep breaths, counted to ten, and tried to calm down. No big deal, she thought, he's just showing her some tricks. But why him? Pres was just as good at lifts, and probably stronger. She looks a little wobbly up there, like a strong wind would topple her. Maybe I should show her how it's done. . . .

"What's wrong, Olivia? Aren't you feeling well?" Olivia had been so preoccupied with watching Walt and Jessica that she hadn't noticed Ardith walking over to her. She jumped when she heard Ardith's voice.

"No — yes — I mean I'm fine," Olivia muttered.

"Then get out on the floor, please. We need all the help we can get."

"Oh . . . sure . . . I was just going to." Olivia's legs felt like lead, but she forced herself to stand up.

"There are a couple of girls who specifically asked for you. They want you to show them some of your gymnastic maneuvers. They're over there." Ardith pointed toward the opposite wall.

"I see them. What're their names?" Olivia wanted to stall for time.

"Sally Cook and Betsey Dodson, and they're very eager to learn. I knew you'd be happy to help them."

"Of course," Olivia lied. The last thing she felt like doing was teaching a couple of newcomers, but she managed to smile.

As she made her way across the gym, Olivia had grim thoughts. Maybe I should give up right now, she wondered. What's the point in wasting my time coaching, training, worrying about tryouts if I've had it with being a cheerleader? There are other things in life. . . .

"Oh, Olivia, we're so glad you've come to help us!" Betsey said sincerely. She was a curly-haired blonde with a sweet smile.

"That's right," Sally said. "We decided you're absolutely the best cheerleader we've ever seen. If I could be just half as good. . . ." Sally was a head taller than Betsey, dark-haired, and she bubbled with enthusiasm.

"Well, I'm sure you can be, but it takes a lot of hard work." Olivia couldn't help but be pleased by their admiration.

"Will you show us how to do a slow cartwheel? I think that's the hardest thing in the world," Betsey said.

"I'd be happy to show you," Olivia answered, and this time she wasn't lying. In fact, she thought, as she stretched her arms over her head, I'd be foolish to make a fast decision about cheerleading. If I stop training now, I'll never have a chance to make the squad again. There's always time later to bow out.

CHAPTER

It was five o'clock and Ardith had to blow her whistle three times in order to get everyone's attention.

"I'm pleased to see how well this has worked out," she said. "From now until the end of May we'll practice Monday, Wednesday, and Friday afternoons. I strongly advise you to attend all these sessions if you are serious about trying out. That doesn't mean you can't work out on the other days as well."

"Will the Varsity Squad be here for the regular sessions?" Betsey asked.

"The Varsity members are committed to keeping in shape and polishing up their routines for Field Day, which will be their last official performance. That means they'll be here, too, and like today, will be available for help. I look forward to seeing all of you on Wednesday."

There was a scattering of applause and excited

comments: "Can't wait till Wednesday!" "I don't think there's enough time for me to practice." "Today was so much fun, I don't care if I make the squad or not." "Sounds like sour grapes." "No, just warding off doom." "Whatever happens, I'm going to practice every chance I get." "Me, too . . . even if it kills me!"

Then the tired participants drifted off to the locker rooms. Sally and Betsey thanked Olivia profusely, told her they didn't want to monopolize her every time, but hoped she'd give them some more tips.

"I promise," Olivia said, and rushed off to the locker room. She knew if she wasn't home at a reasonable hour her mother would be ready to send out a search party. She planned to save time by grabbing her clothes, stuffing them in her canvas bag, and taking a shower at home.

Nancy, Angie, and Mary Ellen were huddled together at the far end of the locker room, obviously talking about the new candidates. "Come join the fun," Mary Ellen called to Olivia, who was running a comb through her hair.

"Can't," Olivia said. "Have to get home." Her friends knew what a worrier Mrs. Evans was, so no further explanation was necessary.

Olivia didn't want to hurry home, but she also didn't want to talk about the hopefuls who were trying out. The three girls, her fellow squad members, were graduating and they could say anything they wanted about the newcomers. But Olivia was a competitor. She didn't want to say anything that sounded self-serving. Better not get involved, she decided, slamming her locker shut and waving good-bye.

Olivia was surprised to see Tara Armstrong on the steps outside the building, since she thought Tara had been the first one to leave the locker room. They exchanged "Hi's" and Tara said, "Going my way?"

"Depends," Olivia answered. "I live on Belmont and Main — three blocks from here."

"I'm going in the same direction. Mind if I join you?"

"No, but I'm kind of in a hurry."

"No problem." Tara fell in step with Olivia and asked, "How'd you think practice went this afternoon?"

"It was okay," Olivia said noncommittally. She was a private person and wasn't going to go into detail about her feelings with someone she hardly knew. "How'd you like it?"

"I liked it a lot, but I would think it'd be kind of boring for you."

"You never know what can happen," Olivia said.

"Aren't the same old routines a drag?"

"There's always the unexpected. . . . Someone might break a leg." Olivia grinned at her own black humor.

"That's something to look forward to," Tara said, laughing along. "But seriously, I would think a year of cheerleading would be plenty, especially when you're the star . . . the way you are."

"Thanks for the compliment."

"If I were you, I'd want to go out in a blaze of glory."

"I'm not sure what you mean," Olivia said slowly.

"I mean, Olivia, that even though you're not the captain of the squad, you do the most dazzling stunts. No one can take their eyes off you. If I were you, I wouldn't want to worry about anyone else taking my place." Tara smiled at Olivia.

"Are you trying to tell me something, Tara?"

"Not at all. In fact, I can't think of anything better than being on the squad with you! You really raise the level of everyone's performance. I just thought you might be suffering from burnout — you know, emotional exhaustion and all that. You look so delicate, I would think you'd want to take it easy your senior year."

"It's a thought, Tara . . . but, oh . . . I don't know."

"The truth is, for my sake, I really hope you'll be on the squad next year. Even if I don't make it, it's so great to watch you. But for your sake . . . well, maybe I shouldn't say it, but I think you should think twice before going through the hassle of trying out."

"It's nice of you to tell me what you think." Olivia was flattered, and even touched by Tara's concern. She had hit a nerve by actually expressing some of Olivia's own doubts, and Tara had a really sweet manner. In fact, it hadn't occurred to anyone else that it might be in Olivia's best interest to forget about cheerleading. Only her mother was against it, but that was because she was so nervous about Olivia's health.

Tara touched Olivia's arm lightly and slowed her pace. "This is where I leave you. I live two blocks away on Elm. It sure was nice talking to you."

"Thanks, Tara. I guess I'll see you Wednesday."

"I hope so." Tara beamed her brilliant smile at Olivia, and added, "Unless you decide not to bother. . . ."

"I still have to train for Field Day," Olivia answered.

"Oh, that's right. Anyhow, I hope we can get together sometime when neither of us has to worry about pulling a muscle."

"I'd like that," Olivia said.

"See you later," Tara said, and ran off.

Olivia watched until Tara was out of sight, and thought about what an unusual girl she was. Besides being exceptional-looking — that red hair made her a standout — she seemed awfully perceptive. Olivia was slow to warm up to people, but Tara was so friendly, it was impossible not to like her. And she obviously had mind-reading abilities. Otherwise, how could she have zeroed in on all the doubts Olivia had been carrying around?

Tara quietly let herself into the Armstrongs' charming white-brick colonial house, waited until she heard the sound of voices, and then swept into the den where her mother was playing bridge. "Hello, everybody," she said gaily.

Tara's mother, Emily, had had a bridge game every Monday afternoon for as long as Tara

25

could remember. So she knew all the women as well as her own family — when she was little, she actually called them her aunts — and they all doted on her.

Tara first singled out her mother, an impeccably groomed auburn-haired woman, kissed her on the cheek, and said, "Hi, Mummy."

"Hello, darling, so glad you're here. Everyone's been hoping you'd get home before they had to leave."

Tara went around the table, and gave each lady an affectionate peck on the cheek.

"Where've you been?" one of them asked.

"Going out for cheerleading. There was a practice session today. In order to even try out, I have to work out three times a week."

"I think all the judges will have to do is take a look at you and you'll make the squad," said another admirer.

Tara smiled modestly. "It's not that easy. There are lots of maneuvers I have to master."

"You're such a good athlete, you don't have to worry," the third lady said.

"I wish you were one of the judges . . . in fact, I wish you all were. Then I wouldn't have to worry at all!" Tara laughed.

Her mother had finished dealing the cards, and Tara took that as her cue to leave. One thing she'd learned as a toddler was not to delay a bridge game more than was necessary.

"Great seeing you all," she said, "but I have to go now. I have tons of homework."

She blew a kiss to everyone and breezed out of the den. But just before she started to climb the stairs to her bedroom, she slowed down. Tara didn't want to miss the remarks that inevitably followed her appearance, and she wasn't disappointed.

"She's such a love!" "Beautiful *and* smart!" "What a wonderful daughter!"

Then her mother summed it all up: "I think we're so lucky. As Joe says, 'We were only blessed with one child, but this one is a winner!' "

Then the bidding began, and Tara slowly climbed the stairs, glowing from what she'd heard. Tara craved constant recognition, feeling that if she were always the center of things, the "winner," her parents would love her and indulge her.

Her father was a corporate lawyer, worked a sixty-hour week, and made a lot of money. His interests, outside of work, were Tara and tennis. He was pleased that his wife was perfectly content to be a housewife whose sole responsibility was to run the home, entertain clients, and keep Tara happy. Since the Armstrongs had a full-time housekeeper — Marie was a middle-aged French woman who had been with the family for ten years — Emily could do all that Joe required of her with ease. And she still had time to indulge her passions for cards, golf, shopping, and occasional volunteer work.

Tara had always gotten her own way about everything — Emily and Joe actually vied with each other to please her — but she was too smart to play the "spoiled brat" role. Instead, she put into effect one of her mother's favorite cliches: "It's easier to catch flies with honey than with vinegar." Tara applied that maxim to all her relationships, and so far it had worked. She was the teacher's pet in elementary school, and in high school she was considered a model student. Marie couldn't do enough for her, from pressing her clothes to making her favorite brownies. Her parents' friends were charmed by her.

Tara didn't have any close girl friends, but that was her choice. She wanted to be liked, if it served her purpose, but she wasn't interested in having a best friend. That meant making too much of an emotional investment. Boys were attracted to her, but she didn't want to be part of a couple. She much preferred flirting and playing games to getting involved with just one guy. And her parents bragged about her army of boyfriends.

Tara closed the door to her room and sank down on the pink and green flowered chair that matched her canopied bedspread and curtains. She sighed wearily as she bent over to unlace her sneakers. It had been a strenuous day, and maintaining a cheerful attitude for her mother's friends hadn't been easy after her encounter with Olivia. Of course she'd planned the whole thing, planting herself on the school steps where she'd be certain to catch her. But she wasn't quite sure how effective she'd been in persuading Olivia not to try out. Well, at least she'd *seemed* to sow some seeds of doubt. . . .

Tara leaned back in her chair and thought about the other most threatening contenders. There was nothing she could do about Jessica Bennett, who was extraordinary. Unless she broke a leg, Jessica would be accepted unanimously. There *had* to be two boys on the squad, so she might as well cross all the males off her worry list. Then there were Hope, Samantha, Holly, Sally, Betsey, and a dozen or so others she'd be up against. It would be impossible to discourage all of them before the tryouts, the way she may have eliminated Olivia. But maybe she could use other means. . . .

Sally and Betsey, she knew, were probably the most determined to be chosen. And they had just enough ability to score high if they worked hard. Tara stood up and stretched luxuriously, a catlike smile curling her lips. *If I could mess up their routines,* she thought, *that'll be two more competitors I can scratch.*

How pleased Mother and Dad will be when I get on the squad, she thought. *I wonder what they'll give me.*

CHAPTER

Nancy, Angie, and Mary Ellen had taken showers, changed their clothes, and strolled out of the building, still talking nonstop. They felt closer than ever, now that the competition was over for them, and they confided in one another that they were enjoying being "mentors."

"It's really fun being on the other side," Nancy remarked. "I like showing others what I've learned."

"Maybe you should become a teacher," Angie suggested.

"Don't get carried away." Nancy chuckled. "I think what I like about this is that I don't have to be scared anymore. I'll never forget how terrified I was at tryouts last year. Now all that's behind me."

"I like getting feedback for my efforts, too," Angie said. "Hope Chang, for example, absorbs everything like a sponge, and she's so appreciative. I consider her my personal protégé."

"Most of the new kids are knocking themselves out," Mary Ellen commented, "except for Samantha. I was demonstrating for her and a few others how to coordinate the cheers with the routines. You know, jumping at the right time when you say the word *up* and finishing your maneuvers when the cheer is over. Everyone agreed it's a lot harder than it looks."

"What did Samantha say?" Nancy asked.

"Nothing — absolutely zilch. She just had a blank look on her face, as though I'd been talking about Einstein's theory of relativity."

"Do you think it's possible to be so beautiful that you don't have to say anything? I mean Samantha has so many guys after her, she's *got* to be conceited," Angie said.

"She definitely comes across as snobby," Nancy agreed. "But I have to admit she looks sensational in that red leotard."

"I just can't figure out why she even wants to be on the squad. She acts like it's beneath her," Mary Ellen said.

"Don't be so sure," Angie cautioned. "If she really felt that way, she wouldn't bother. Maybe she has some problems we don't know about."

"Angie," Mary Ellen said, "you are so incredible — always seeing the good side of people."

"Well, why not, Melon?"

"You're right, I know. And that's why you should become a social worker. You've got everything it takes."

"I plan to, you know. And you've got every-

31

thing it takes to be a model, if that's what you want."

"And what have I got?" Nancy asked.

Mary Ellen and Angie frowned at Nancy, then looked at each other, and shrugged their shoulders hopelessly.

"Thanks a lot," Nancy growled, and the three of them burst out laughing.

"You know," Angie said, "we've had our ups and downs on the squad, but it's all been worthwhile. It's made us such good friends."

"It's too bad Olivia can't share this with us," Nancy said. "If only she were graduating, too. . . ."

"I'm glad she isn't!" Mary Ellen exclaimed. "She'll carry on the tradition of everything we've worked for."

"You're right," Angie agreed. "Because of Olivia, we'll know the Tarenton cheerleaders will continue to be the greatest!"

"I never thought of it that way," Nancy said. "Being a member of the squad will be one of my fondest memories of Tarenton, and leaving it won't be so horrible, knowing that one of us will still be on it."

Hope Chang should have been encouraged by the afternoon's practice. She'd done exceptionally well with all the moves that Angie had demonstrated. Angie had taken several newcomers under her wing, but none of them had caught on as quickly and performed as expertly as Hope, and Peter Rayman. On the way to the locker room, Angie had whispered to Hope that she was a "natural."

"Thanks, Angie," Hope had said, smiling.

Hope was good at everything she did, even those things she wasn't particularly interested in, like cheerleading. She was an "A" student, an excellent reporter for the school paper, and a fine violinist. All these pursuits she thoroughly enjoyed, but going out for the cheerleading squad was a low priority. Even though she was a "natural," as Angie had said, she'd rather have been home reading a book or practicing the violin.

Hope went around the back of the Chang's contemporary house, and entered through the kitchen door. The family had moved from the East after her father, who was a doctor, had taken a position at the Haven Lake Medical Center where he taught and practiced orthopedic medicine. Her younger brother, James, was in fifth grade, and her older brother, William, was a freshman at the University of Wisconsin. Mrs. Chang, a petite woman with a delightful but firm manner, was a painter who specialized in watercolor scenes. She worked in a studio on the side wing of the house that had northern light. After five, she could usually be found in the kitchen preparing dinner.

Mrs. Chang was putting an apple pie in the oven when Hope came through the back door.

"Hello, dear," she said as she closed the oven door and turned to embrace her daughter. "How'd it go?"

"Hello, Mother. It was fine," Hope replied.

"I'm sure you did splendidly."

"I did okay."

Mrs. Chang gently put her hand on Hope's shoulder and smiled at her. "Come sit down," she said, and guided her to a chair beside the butcher-block table where the family always ate breakfast together.

"Look," she began, after they both sat down, "we went over all this before, and your father and I both believe you should participate in some extracurricular sport."

"Yes, Mother," Hope answered, staring at the floor.

"You know, when I was your age, I would have given anything to have been a cheerleader. When I went to my first football game and saw these girls in their bright blue outfits, waving pompons and prancing and cheering — no boy cheerleaders in those days — I thought it was the most thrilling sight imaginable. I'm so happy you're in a school where it's possible."

"I know, Mother, and that's why I'm going out for it . . . and I'm really trying to make the squad." Hope gazed out of the window.

"I know you are, Hope. You've never disappointed us." Her mother pushed back her chair, indicating the discussion was over.

"Do you need me to help in the kitchen?" Hope asked.

"No thanks. Everything's almost finished. . . . We're having your favorite tonight — fried chicken, which I made first thing this morning. I know you want to practice your violin."

"That's for sure!" Hope exclaimed.

She waited politely until her mother stood up because it would have been rude to rush off. Then she hurried to her room, which made maximum use of limited space. Against one wall was an ivory-colored unit that combined a desk, book-shelves, and cabinets. The daybed and bolsters, covered in a soft shade of green, served as a sofa, and vertical off-white blinds covered the windows.

The room was impeccably neat, because Hope had been trained to make her bed and put away her things as soon as she was big enough to do so. She was shocked and amused when she visited other girls and saw their messy rooms. They didn't seem to care in the least that they had to waste time rummaging through piles of clothing and papers to find whatever they were looking for.

Hope pulled her music stand and violin out of the closet and thought about how her parents had pressured her to try out for the squad. An obedient daughter, she would never go against her parents' wishes. Besides, her mother and father were good to her, and she loved them very much. Also, she honestly believed they knew what was best for her. She had to admit, it really had been kind of fun when Angie asked her and Peter Rayman to demonstrate a series of frog leaps.

Hope had never really noticed Peter before. They had a few classes together, but he kept a very low profile, never asking questions or volunteering to talk unless he was called upon. Today they had hardly exchanged two words, but every time she glanced in his direction she caught him staring at her. And then, if she wasn't mistaken, she perceived a faint blush on his cheeks — a blush that had nothing to do with exercise.

Hope took some sheet music out of her cabinet, spread it on the music stand, and then tuned her violin. She smiled as she thought how reluctant she felt about going out for the squad. But once again, maybe her parents *did* know what was best!

Jessica wasn't sure herself how it happened, but after practice she found herself being escorted home by two boys: Walt and Sean. Walt knew that Olivia had to hurry home, so he didn't feel guilty about not being with her. He did have a little trouble justifying why he immediately took the opportunity to be with Jessica. Walt admitted to himself that he found her very attractive. Obviously, Sean did, too.

Walt and Sean outdid themselves trying to impress Jessica. She was a good listener, laughed easily, and appeared to enjoy both of them. Jessica was relaxed with boys, possibly because she had two older brothers who, until recently, treated her as the "kid sister." But in spite of their constant teasing, it was obvious her brothers thought she was great. They had taught her to throw a ball like a boy, they appreciated her good sense of humor, and their friends liked her.

Walt began telling Jessica about his family's TV talk show, which she said her family watched every morning.

"Why don't you do a feature on cheerleading?" Sean asked.

"I've already thought of that," Walt answered.

"My folks agreed it might be a very entertaining segment."

"I'd be happy to offer you my services," Sean said.

"I'll keep that in the back of my mind," Walt told him, not sure whether Sean was putting him on or not.

"I've had a little experience in front of the camera," Sean went on.

"Oh really!" Jessica looked at him admiringly. "What did you do?"

"Not one of your major movies, Jessica, but I did a commercial for a sports equipment company. It was a lot of fun, and paid well. All I had to do was wear some tennis clothes, hold onto a racquet, and flash my teeth."

Jessica appraised him from head to toe. "I bet you're very photogenic."

Walt ground his teeth, thinking he was definitely losing the first round. "What I had in mind for a cheerleading piece was something a little more creative. We don't just want the socko-jocko image."

"It's hard to be something you're not," Sean explained.

Walt hadn't felt competitive about a girl in so long, he was surprised at his ridiculous impulse to punch Sean out. Besides, he had a good, year-long relationship with Olivia, and this flirtation with Jessica was just a momentary transgression . . . or was it? There had been too much verbal fencing with Sean for Walt to know if anything was happening between Jessica and Sean.

"This is where I live," Jessica said, stopping

in front of a tree-shaded, red brick house. "I'd ask you both in for a snack, but it's too close to dinner. Another time, okay?"

"Sure, any time," Sean said before Walt could get a word in.

"Don't forget what I told you about how to balance on your shoulders. I'll be available whenever you want to refine our act." Walt was determined to say something that would exclude Sean.

"That'd be great, Walt. I'll let you know."

Jessica smiled warmly, waved at both of them, and walked up the path to her house.

Sean and Walt were left standing there.

Sean finally broke the awkward silence. "Going my way?"

"Which way is that?" Walt asked.

Sean pointed east, which happened to be the direction of Walt's house. He couldn't have been more on target, but Walt wasn't in the mood for any more sparring.

"Have to stop off at the store," he lied, just in case Sean knew where he lived.

"See you," Sean said. "I think I'll jog home — helps keep the bod in shape." He patted his stomach and laughed.

"Ciao," Walt said, and strode off in the opposite direction.

Walt was confused and bothered by Jessica, and baffled by his reaction to Sean. He'd always been resilient, clowning around even when he was feeling low. His relationship with Olivia had seemed so solid, but now he wasn't sure about anything.

CHAPTER

Patrick Henley pulled his garbage truck into the Mobil station on Main Street where he regularly filled up with gas and oil. It was four o'clock on Saturday afternoon and he had just finished his rounds. Working three days a week after school, and almost all day on Saturday, was nothing new to Patrick. It naturally cut into most extracurricular activities he might participate in, but he still found time to be the official school photographer. Also, there were definite compensations to his job: He owned his own truck and was making money to put into the moving business he operated with Pres Tilford. He certainly knew what his future would be.

Patrick's friends always said that he was perfectly suited for his trash collecting because he had a muscular build, just right for the job. Patrick was secure and easygoing, and agreed with the description. He was exceptionally strong and demanded respect partly because of his size, but also because of his total lack of pretension and his ability to laugh at himself.

The one person in the world who upset his balance was Mary Ellen. Patrick was in love with her and honestly believed he always would be in spite of what he considered her distorted values. Mary Ellen dated other boys from time to time, not because she liked them more than Patrick, but because they came from wealthy families or were headed for big professional careers. Still, she could never quite hide the fact that she was irresistibly drawn to Patrick.

On as many occasions as possible, Patrick arranged to be alone with Mary Ellen, and then they kissed each other longingly. It was both painful and ironic to Patrick that Mary Ellen allowed him to hold her in his arms, presumably shutting out the world, and then have her pull away. Patrick knew that the idea of going on a date with him, which meant being picked up in a garbage truck, was appalling to her. And to kiss with any passion in such a setting was . . . well, nearly impossible. He knew that Mary Ellen's feelings for him were stronger than they were for anyone else, but that she couldn't see herself going with a garbage man — even if he made a pile of money.

Patrick glanced in the rearview mirror as he waited for the attendant to fill up his tank, and noticed a familiar red Porsche a hair's breadth away from his back fender. He leapt out of his truck and frantically waved his arms to the driver, who happened to be Preston Tilford III.

"Sir, do you know what you're doing?" Patrick

asked, as though they had never met before. "This happens to be my most precious possession," he said, patting his truck, "and also the key to my livelihood."

"I had no idea . . ." Pres answered teasingly, as he stuck his head out the car window. "I thought it was . . . well, a garbage truck."

"It's that, too," Patrick admitted, and then they both laughed.

"What are you doing here?" Pres asked.

"Same thing you are, I would guess. Have to keep tanked up, or we're out of business. Next pickup day is Monday, but I don't like to worry about not having enough gas. What about you? Going for a joyride?"

"You might call it that. Actually, I was going to take a spin to cool off."

"Who are you mad at?"

"My folks, for a change."

"Sorry to hear it. The usual problem?"

"Hey buddy," the rumpled, bearded gas attendant interrupted, "I know it's tea time, but I've got work to do. Pay me twelve bucks, please, and move it."

"Oh, sorry about that." Patrick pulled out his wallet, peeled off some bills, and handed them to the attendant.

"Listen, Patrick," Pres said, "why don't you dump your truck and I'll tell you all about it. I'll follow you to your garage."

"Sure thing. I might suffer from culture shock, though. The difference between your clean lean sports car, and my mean green truck. . . ."

"Don't give me that stuff, Patrick. The only

41

person I know who's more hung up than me on his means of transportation is you."

"Meet me at the garage," Patrick said, chuckling. "I think the contrast will do me good."

Pres waited on the street in the Porsche and watched Patrick roll his truck into the garage, and then make sure the garage doors were securely locked.

"All set," Patrick said, as he trotted over to the car and slid into the bucket seat on the passenger side.

"You treat that heap of metal like a baby," Pres joked.

"I put it to bed for the weekend. No point in taking chances . . . there might be a freak snowstorm."

"Only kidding. Actually, from the passenger seat, it's always looked fun to drive." Pres revved up the motor, and took off.

"Doesn't have the personality this does," Patrick said slowly, "but I think it has more character."

"Right now, that's what I need."

"Where are we going, by the way?"

"Thought we'd take a drive around the lake. I've got to work off some steam," Pres said firmly.

"You said it was the usual argument with your parents. You should be used to it by now."

"I should be, but it's getting worse because I'll be graduating soon. According to my father, the moment of truth is upon me."

"Whatever that's supposed to mean." Patrick never pretended to know something he didn't.

"In this case, it means that if I don't go to Princeton like my father and grandfather, there'll be hell to pay. And if I don't take advantage of this summer to prepare for my future at Tarenton Fabricators, I might be disowned," Pres explained.

"Meaning you'll be cut off from the family fortune?" Patrick asked.

Pres nodded. "Exactly."

"That seems extreme."

"I know," Pres agreed, "but maybe giving up the money is worth it if otherwise the rest of my life means one gigantic hassle with my parents, or going into a business that I can't stand. It's not that I'm opposed to business, but the idea of working for my father is a total turn-off. I can't see just sitting in an office in a three-piece suit, worrying about what's cost-effective, trimming budgets, and balancing accounts — with the elder Preston breathing down my neck and telling me I'm doing it wrong."

Patrick thought for a minute. "I can't see you doing that, either. You're more the physical type."

"I tried to explain that to my father and his answer was I could play squash a few times a week at the racquet club. He really doesn't understand anything." Pres speeded up, angrily palming the wheel, and skidded dangerously around a curb. It was his way of taking out his frustration, but it made Patrick gasp in alarm.

"Take it easy, Pres. No point in wrecking the Porsche, to say nothing of what you might do to us."

Pres slowed down and shook his head despairingly. "I'm sorry," he apologized. "I shouldn't be dumping my problems on you."

"Don't worry about that. I'd like to think of a way out for you. . . . I suppose you have to have an alternative plan."

"Like what?" Pres asked.

"Well, what is it you really want to do? Doctor, lawyer, bum . . . ?"

"None of the above. I'm not sure, but I think I'd like to keep on working with something that has wheels."

"I can't see you as a used-car salesman," Patrick joked.

"Me, neither."

"Test pilot?"

"I'm not that brave."

"Good Humor man?"

"Closer."

"I'm running out of ideas . . . unless . . . unless. . . ."

"Unless what?"

"I just had a brainstorm. How'd you like to expand our moving business — make it the biggest and best in Tarenton, to be exact? I've always thought we could do it, but I never guessed you were interested."

Pres glanced at Patrick to see if he was serious, and from the look on his face Pres was certain he was. "*Interested*? I had your brainstorm a long time ago. It's just that, well, you already know about my dad. . . ."

"I think you can still give your dad what he wants and do you're own thing, too," Patrick said, turning to look directly at Pres.

"What do you mean?"

"Just explain to him that we're going to make the company grow," Patrick said eagerly. "We'll buy another truck, drum up more business, maybe even hire some people. Show your dad you're a businessman, even though you're not going into the *family* business."

"Hey," Pres said excitedly, "I think this is a terrific idea. I even think we could afford another truck soon. My grandfather has promised me a reasonably large check when I graduate. I could use some of the money for the wheels, and live on the rest till we really got rolling."

"That would be great. It would temporarily solve your financial problem."

"Can you see my old man's face when I tell him I want to be a *moving* man, full time?" Pres laughed out loud for the first time all afternoon.

"Call yourself a relocation engineer, and he might just go for it."

CHAPTER

6

It was the second week of cheerleading practice and the less serious contenders, or those who knew they were totally outclassed, had withdrawn from the training program.

"We're down to the hard core," Ardith announced at the beginning of the session on Wednesday. "I want to remind you that the day of the tryouts, each of you will be asked to perform an individual routine that should show some originality. I suggest you work up something and practice it daily. You will be judged on inventiveness as well as execution. Even though the squad must perform as smoothly as a single body, there is room for individual expression."

"You mean, Mrs. Engborg, that six of us could make a pyramid, but the one on top might do a special stunt like a flip twist on the way down?" Tara asked.

46

"Precisely. Thank you, Tara, for that clear explanation."

Holly Hudson looked daggers at Tara. She wished she'd been the one to speak up first. She didn't like anyone getting ahead of her.

"Are there any other questions or comments?" Ardith waited and looked around the gym.

"Last time you said we should try to think up some new cheers," Holly piped up. "I have one ready for you."

"That's fine. We'd love to hear it."

Holly pranced into the center of the gym, obviously enjoying the opportunity to show off. "I thought you'd like this one . . . and you have my permission to use it. I personally think you should, because . . . well, you'll see."

Then Holly plunged into a series of energetic moves, and at the same time shouted breathlessly:

"When you're up, you're up!
When you're down, you're down!
When you're up against Tarenton,
You're upside down!"

Then Holly took a deep bow, milking the audience for applause which might have been much more spirited if she hadn't come on so strong.

"Thank you, Holly," Ardith said. "That was excellent. We might add it to our repertoire."

"I think you should, Mrs. Engborg," Holly said with assurance. "The squad needs some fresh material. Actually, I dream up these cheers all the time, so I'll have others for you."

Nancy, who was sitting with Angie, Mary Ellen, and Olivia, whispered, "I wonder who dreamed her up?"

The four of them tried to suppress a fit of laughter. Then Angie, turning to Olivia, said, "It is a good cheer, though, and you could do great things with it, Livvy."

"Could I?" Olivia didn't want to say what she was thinking — that just the thought of working out a new routine made her bone-tired.

"All right, people," Ardith was saying, "let's get started. I want you to begin firming up the routine that you plan to present on 'Judgment Day.' I think you should work on that for twenty minutes while I coach the Varsity members in their Field Day routine." Then she blew her whistle, which meant she was ready for the action to begin.

"Where does that leave me?" Olivia mumbled to the girls as they headed towards Ardith. "How am I supposed to work on my tryout cheer and also on the Field Day routine?"

"You're so good, you can do both," Nancy assured her.

"Not at the same time," Olivia groaned.

"You can work on your own tryout material anytime," Mary Ellen said.

"That's right," Angie affirmed. "You've got the experience that none of the others have."

"Nobody understands," Olivia murmured in such a low voice that she couldn't be heard.

Olivia was annoyed that the other cheerleaders weren't aware of how torn she was. Ardith, who was usually tuned into the mood of her athletes, seemed to take for granted that Olivia could handle whatever was required of her. As if to confirm that opinion, Ardith said, "We're going to work on the spin top. The boys will lift Olivia in the air while the girls cartwheel around the formation."

When Olivia heard that, she felt a sharp pain in her stomach that traveled to her chest and made her breathe fast. It was an odd sensation, and passed quickly. She didn't want to pay any attention to it, because if her mother found out that she had the slightest suggestion of pain around her heart, she'd whisk her into the hospital emergency room. Olivia wanted to avoid that, so she mustered all her strength and executed the spin expertly.

While the Varsity members were refining their routine, the new candidates were developing their own acts. Tara took the opportunity to corner Betsey Dodson and show her a sprint and back walkover that ended in a dramatic high jump.

"That's terrific," Betsey complimented her. "I wish I could use that in my routine, but that wouldn't be fair."

Tara touched Betsey's arm lightly. "I'll release it, Betsey, because I'm not going to use it. I have something else planned."

"You mean it? I think it would make a great ending."

"That's what I think, too. You can have it."

"Fantastic! Thanks, Tara."

"I've got to practice some handstands against the wall now. See you later," Tara said and ran off.

"Thanks again for everything," Betsey called after her, and then immediately went to work on the new stunt.

Tara was pleased that Betsey was so susceptible to her suggestion. That meant half of her problem was solved. Now if she could only manage to get Sally Cook alone, show her the same moves, and have her plan to use them, too, she was sure she could scratch those two girls off her competition list. The judges would think it suspicious that two candidates had the identical endings to their routines. Hadn't Mrs. Engborg said she was looking for "*individual expression*"?

It would have been too obvious for Tara to seek out Sally right away. Besides, Ardith was blowing her whistle, which meant everyone had to stop what they were doing and go on to something else. "I want to work out some choreography with you," she said. "This requires razor-sharp synchronization, which the Varsity members will demonstrate."

Mary Ellen led the cheerleaders in a series of intricate moves, and Tara realized that Mary Ellen, as leader of the squad, might have a few tips that would benefit her. When practice was over, Tara sidled up to her, complimented her on how she combined subtlety and authority, and asked innocently what special advice she could give her.

"Thanks," Mary Ellen responded, pleased that Tara had sought her out. "I think the important thing is to get all the routines down pat, so that they become second nature. *Then* you can polish them. If you have to think too hard about whether you're doing everything right, you'll make cheering look too much like work. As Ardith says, we're supposed to be cheerleaders, not drearleaders."

"I see what you mean," Tara said. "That's good advice. If you think of anything else, will you let me know?"

"Why, sure. Actually, I think you'll do fine, Tara. You've got the right personality, which is something nobody can teach."

"Thanks, Mary Ellen. That's really nice of you."

They strolled into the locker room together, and Tara was thinking how smart she was to get friendly with Mary Ellen. Not that Mary Ellen had any influence with the judges, but she might just need Mary Ellen to work out some wrinkles that she had in her tryout routine. It certainly didn't hurt to have the Varsity Cheerleaders on her side.

Nancy Goldstein had a civilized relationship with her parents, and tried to live up to their standards. That didn't mean that she didn't have occasional disagreements, especially with her father, who was just as strong-minded as his daughter. But she wasn't rebellious by nature, and her home life was generally smooth.

They hadn't had any major arguments lately, especially because it was assumed that Nancy would go to Brown University, where she already had early acceptance. The fight Nancy had had with her boyfriend Eric Campbell about her not going to the community college where he was a coach had only been patched up because Nancy had said she'd reconsider about Brown. But she hadn't told her parents that.

At dinner that night, which was served in the Goldsteins' dining room, her mother suggested that Nancy have a graduation party.

"It would be so nice to have all your friends here for a buffet," her mother generously offered.

"And a swim, weather permitting," Mr. Goldstein added. "I'd like to get some mileage out of the pool."

"That's really nice of you," Nancy said. "But there are so many parties planned around the senior class, I'm not sure anyone will be interested in another one."

"Well, keep it in mind," Mrs. Goldstein said. "You've done so well at Tarenton — and getting into Brown was such a wonderful accomplishment — that we'd like you to have a special celebration."

"Thanks a lot, Mother. I'll think about it."

"Let me know soon, because even though there's time before tryouts, I'll have to arrange for the food."

"I'll let you know soon, don't worry."

"Going to check it out with your twelve best friends, I bet," her father said.

Nancy laughed. "You're a mind reader, Dad. That's exactly what I plan to do."

"If you prefer a luncheon with just girls, Nancy,

we could do that instead," her mother interrupted.

"Are you kidding? A party without boys isn't a party," replied Nancy.

"I just aim to please. So let me know," Mrs. Goldstein said.

As soon as dinner was over, Nancy went upstairs to her room. She pulled out her journal which she'd written in daily since eighth grade. When she first began keeping a diary, the entries read a little bit like a newscaster's report — and not a very exciting one. Typically, she would list the day's events: "Had a history test. Knew most of the answers, thank goodness. If I get an A in the course, it will bring up my average and I'll get on the honor roll. Let's hope!" Or, "Tom Butler is sooooo cute. He's in ninth grade, and probably thinks I'm too young for anything, but he said 'Hi' to me in the hall. That means he knows I'm alive!"

It wasn't until tenth grade that Nancy had started recording her feelings, too. When she scanned the old entries, she realized how far she had come . . . and how much she had grown, especially after leaving her school in Ohio and coming to Tarenton High in the eleventh grade.

In spite of her dark good looks and intelligence, she'd felt isolated from the other girls who had been classmates together for years. Then, after making the cheerleading squad, everything had fallen into place. She'd made lots of girl friends, had several brief romances; her most serious one, with Ben Adamson, had ended tragically with his accidental death on a mountain-climbing expedition. The shock was devastating, but Nancy had recovered and had dedicated herself to helping others at a rehabilitation center. It was there she met Eric, a physical therapist, who coached the handicapped and was earning his degree at the local junior college.

Eric was quiet, earnest, good-looking, and Nancy was definitely attracted to him. But to tell the truth, Nancy wasn't sure if Eric was the one for her.

Now that the year was winding up, she'd have to make some hard decisions about her future. . . . Tell Eric that she had definitely decided to go away to college, which meant the end of their steady dating, or opt for staying at home, enrolling at the local junior college, and continuing their relationship. Lately, almost everything she wrote in her journal related to this problem. Better than boring her friends, Nancy thought.

Tonight she had something else to think about — something much less serious and a lot more fun — and that was the party her mother had suggested. *That* was a problem she would enjoy sharing with her friends. Her best friends were her co-cheerleaders, and they often gravitated together in the cafeteria for lunch. That would be the perfect time to sound them out on whether a graduation party was a good idea.

"Your place is so great for a party," Angie said, digging into her yogurt.

"Especially if you want to go swimming and risk getting pneumonia," Mary Ellen chuckled.

Olivia hadn't said anything, although Nancy had brought up the subject of having a graduation party as soon as the four of them had brought their trays to their usual round table near the window.

"Problem is, there are so many graduation parties at the end of the year. Besides the senior prom and the senior picnic, there will be a million private parties," Nancy pointed out. "What do you think, Olivia?"

"Really, Livvy, you haven't said a word," Mary Ellen said.

"Why should I? I'm not graduating," she replied glumly.

"But you know you'd be invited! Just because it's called a graduation party, doesn't mean you can't come. It won't be etched in stone that only seniors are allowed," Nancy emphasized.

"Maybe it should be. I mean, you'll all be talking about going to college or out into the real world, and I'll be stuck in Tarenton. . . ." Olivia's eyes misted.

Nancy, Angie, and Mary Ellen stared at her in amazement. It hadn't occurred to any of them that Olivia felt that way.

"I have a brilliant idea," Angie exclaimed. "Instead of a graduation party, why don't you make it a cheerleader mixer, Nancy. Ardith keeps telling us how important it is to help the new kids who are trying out . . . be friendly and all that stuff."

"Good thinking," Nancy said slowly. "In fact, I think it's a terrific idea!"

"So do I," Mary Ellen agreed. "You can still invite whoever you want."

"Of course, and we'll have some new faces, too," Nancy said. "We'll have it a lot sooner, so it doesn't conflict with any of the senior blasts. What do you say to that, Olivia?"

Olivia nodded her head and tried hard to smile. Her friends were really being nice and she didn't want to seem ungrateful. It wasn't *their* fault that no matter what Nancy's party was called, she'd still feel like an outsider.

CHAPTER

It took some delicate diplomacy on Nancy's part to convince her parents that she wanted a cheerleading mixer in two weeks, rather than a fancy graduation party sometime in May. She brought up the idea at breakfast the next morning, just as her father was finishing his second cup of coffee.

"Oh no," Mrs. Goldstein cried. "That gives me practically no time at all for preparations."

"My friends don't care about gourmet cooking, Mother. As long as there's enough junk food, a variety of soft drinks, and a high-cal dessert, they'll be delirious."

"*I care*, dear. Potato chips and pretzels aren't my idea of what should be served at a party."

"I don't know why you're still so hung up on cheerleading," Mr. Goldstein remarked. "The season's over."

"Being a cheerleader has been a very important

57

part of my life, Dad, and I'll always — "

"All right, all right, Nancy. But if the party's in two weeks, there's no way you can use the pool."

"I know, but we can still dance on the patio. I'll get the squad to decorate it, using a cheerleading theme. It'll be the most original bash of the year — much more fun than the usual graduation party."

Nancy's parents shook their heads and smiled weakly, finally convinced that if they didn't go along with their daughter's wishes, there wouldn't be a party at all.

"Well, if that's what you want," said her mother. "I suppose it will be an easy party to plan. . . ."

"Oh, Mother, I knew you'd see it my way. It really will be the party of the year!"

"Nancy," her father said, pushing back his chair from the breakfast room table, "I think you should become a lawyer. I've known a lot of litigators in my life, but none of them are better than you when it comes to the art of persuasion!"

Nancy's first class was sociology, and since Ms. Connors' lectures were based on the previous day's assignment, Nancy didn't have to concentrate too much. She took a seat in the back of the room, bent her head over her notebook, and appeared to be taking copious notes.

Since she was such a good student, it didn't occur to Ms. Connors that Nancy was totally oblivious to what she was saying. If she'd bothered to glance over Nancy's shoulder, she would have been surprised to see a long roster of names, followed by checks, question marks, and cross-outs. In her organized way, Nancy was planning the guest list.

The couples she would invite were obvious: Nancy and Eric, Walt and Olivia, Angie and Chris, Mary Ellen and Patrick — in spite of her protestations, everyone thought of Mary Ellen and Patrick as "going together" — Pres and someone. Then there were the fresh faces, which included Hope, Sean, Rob, Tara, Peter, Holly, Samantha, Jessica, Carla, Betsey, and Sally, plus many of the Tarenton team players, and about a dozen others who didn't necessarily have a direct connection to the Varsity Squad.

Nancy studied the list and rather reluctantly added Vanessa's name. Vanessa could be such a troublemaker, but by not being invited she might be tempted to do something really harmful.

The one name Nancy decided to scratch was Samantha's. Samantha hadn't spoken to her or any of the other girls on Varsity since practice began. If she was that aloof, she'd be a real drag at a party. Besides, she probably wouldn't accept the invitation anyway.

At lunch that day, Nancy told her friends how she'd convinced her parents to have a cheerleading party the first Saturday in April, less than two weeks away. They all got excited about it, and even Olivia couldn't help but be affected by the others' enthusiasm. Then Nancy showed them the guest list, and they joked about how it could be improved by eliminating some of the prettier girls, and adding some attractive boys who had been overlooked.

"What'll I do for invitations?" Nancy asked.

"Why not a cheer?" Mary Ellen suggested.

"Like what?"

"Well, something that rhymes with bash."

"Cash, mash, sash . . ." Angie offered.

"One of our best cheers starts 'Chica chica boo' — maybe we could do something with that," Olivia said.

"I've got it!" Mary Ellen exclaimed. "Chica chica boo/ Chica chica crash/ You're invited to Nancy Goldstein's/ For a cheerleaders' bash!"

"That's terrific! Worthy of Holly, although I'm sure she wouldn't think so," Nancy said.

"I see you're inviting her," Mary Ellen said, hinting that she wouldn't have been on *her* guest list.

"She's bossy, but at least she talks to us, which is more than I can say for Samantha. Not that Samantha would want to come. . . ."

"Want us to help write out the invitations?" Angie asked. "The four of us could get them done . . . four times as fast."

"That would be wonderful. Will you come to my house after school? I have some plain paper and envelopes, which is all we need."

"I can do it," Mary Ellen said.

"How about you, Olivia?" Nancy asked.

Olivia hesitated before answering. Again, she was feeling a little torn. She didn't want to be left out, but the three seniors were so tight now . . . had so much in common.

"Come on," Angie urged her. "You could do some artistic embellishments — draw six adorable cheerleaders around the edges. You're a good artist!"

"Okay," Olivia said finally. "I'll come."

"That's great. Meet me on the steps after school and we'll all go together."

The four girls were so absorbed in their plans that they didn't notice Walt and Pres until the boys were practically on top of them.

"Looks like a summit meeting here. We've been trying to get your attention for fifteen minutes," Walt said. "We figured you were up to something."

"Tell the truth, what are you planning?" Pres asked.

"A party," Nancy said. "A cheerleaders' bash."

"And we're number one on the guest list, I presume," Pres said.

"Of course," Nancy replied.

"I hope you're inviting some of the new talent," Walt commented in an offhand manner.

"I plan to," Nancy said.

Olivia didn't like Walt's question at all. It could only mean one thing — that he was interested in seeing Jessica in a social situation. Olivia was tempted to ask him why he cared who was there as long as she was, but that would have been childish.

"Sounds great. Anything we can do?" Pres offered.

"We were going to work on the invitations after school today. Want to come over and lend a hand? Since the party's in two weeks, I want to get them out right away."

"I'm available," Pres answered.

"I'm not," Walt said. "Sorry."

"What are you doing, Walt?" Pres asked. "What could be more important than helping these damsels in distress?"

"I'm helping some other damsel, who asked me specifically to show her some routines that require a strong man."

"Where was I when all this was going on? Am I considered the Varsity Wimp?" Pres was so secure about his effect on girls that he could afford to joke about himself.

"It's nothing personal. Just that I was working with Jessica before, and she wanted some extra practice."

Olivia felt that awful painful sensation again, and she clutched the table until it passed, hoping no one noticed.

"Okay, Walt," Pres continued, "if you want to leave me with these four beautiful women — that's your choice."

"I really would like to help you, but I'm already committed. Anyhow, if you need me for some heavy work later, like swinging from the chandeliers in order to decorate the place, let me know, Nancy."

"Thanks, Walt. I just might use your services."

"I aim to please, you know."

The bell rang then, which meant lunch period was over.

"I've got to get my math book out of my locker, so I've got to run. I'll call you later,

Livvy." Walt put his hand on Olivia's shoulder and patted her as if she were a pet dog, she thought. "Don't get writer's cramp," he admonished all of them, and ran off.

Olivia tried to look normal, but her heart was beating a mile a minute. Her friends were jabbering away, but all she could think of was Walt's saying, "I'm helping some other damsel in distress. . . . I'm already committed."

Then why does he even bother to call me later? she wondered. Maybe because he really *does* think of me as a pet dog, and that's his way of tossing me a bone.

CHAPTER

For the next week all anyone talked about was Nancy's upcoming party. Even before the invitations were received, the news spread. There was constant buzzing about it in the halls, the classrooms, the locker rooms. The party took on an aura that surprised even Nancy.

Ardith received her invitation the day of the next practice session. Before the warm-ups began, she pulled Nancy aside and thanked her profusely for including her.

"I'm really flattered, Nancy, but that's the same night of my brother's birthday celebration. Why do all good things happen at once?"

"Maybe you could drop in for a little while." Nancy knew that as a coach, Ardith could be hard as nails, but underneath she had a fun-loving spirit and would definitely be a good addition to the party.

"If I can possibly swing it, I will. You know

how much the cheerleaders mean to me, and how important it is to help the new squad be inspired by the old. I understand you've invited everyone, which is exactly what I would have hoped for."

"I wish you could be there."

"I'll try to stop in."

"That would be great."

"I'll see what I can do. Now we'd better get started."

Ardith assumed her sergeant-at-arms stance, blew one long blast on her whistle, and shouted, "Playtime is over, troops. Let's start out with twenty-five sit-ups. Spread out, everybody." She waited a full sixty seconds while everyone assumed the proper position, then called, "Down-up-down-up—keep those knees straight—down-up-down-up. . . ."

The demands Ardith made during the warm-ups became increasingly more strenuous. After twenty minutes of exercising, executing specific moves seemed like a rest period.

When the session was over, the four Varsity girls took their time cooling off and getting dressed. Ever since the invitations had been sent, they checked daily to hear who had accepted.

"What's the latest tally?" Mary Ellen asked as she fluffed up her hair. Even though it was disheveled from the workout, Mary Ellen looked like she belonged on a magazine cover.

"So far, thirty-nine acceptances." Nancy beamed.

"Any declines?"

"Ardith won't be able to show for long because it's her brother's birthday. But even *she's* going to put in an appearance."

"That's great," Angie said. "I want to hear more, but Chris is waiting for me. He's been so busy working on the yearbook that we've hardly seen each other."

"Only every Friday and Saturday night, and Sunday," Olivia teased.

Angie laughed because she knew it was true, but it didn't mean she didn't want to be with him other times as well. Angie had had crushes before, but this was the first time she had fallen in love. Chris Page, who was probably the most extraordinary-looking guy in the senior class, had flipped for Angie the first time he set eyes on her. He had come to Tarenton as a junior, and every girl in the class had tried to interest him.

Angie liked Chris as a person, not just because he was handsome, and that made her even more desirable in his eyes. He was sensitive, wrote poetry, and for the first time a girl wasn't just hung up on his looks alone. At first, Angie couldn't believe it when he told her he was in love with her, but when it finally sank in, she was just as smitten as he was.

"What brings you two together in the middle of the week?" Mary Ellen asked.

"Chris has asked me to decide which cover I like best for the yearbook. The editorial staff is divided and he wants some input from an objective outsider."

"Just an excuse to get together, I bet," Mary Ellen said, smiling.

"Probably," Angie admitted happily. "Anyhow, my true love awaits. I'll call you later." Then she rushed out.

"They have got to be the luckiest couple," Nancy sighed. "Seems to be a problem-free romance. Not like mine with Eric."

"And certainly not like mine with Patrick. Much as I like Patrick, well, you know. . . ." Mary Ellen spoke in a soft voice and didn't finish her sentence. She didn't want the whole world to hear about her private life.

Olivia was the only one within earshot, and she felt compelled to say something. Lately, her friends had commented on how distracted she'd been, and she decided to make an extra effort to be in tune.

"They are the perfect couple," Olivia remarked.

"So are you and Walt, Olivia," Nancy said. "It's me and Mary Ellen who are having all the love problems."

"Sure, you're really the bachelor types." Olivia wanted to keep the conversation off of her and Walt.

Mary Ellen had finished dressing and sat down dejectedly on the bench beside her locker. The place was emptying out, so she felt free to talk. "My problem is I know exactly the kind of guy I'd like to go with, and I've even met a few that fulfill my qualifications. But I never can fall in love with them."

"Something to do with chemistry," Olivia said. "Either you're drawn together or you're not." She didn't say aloud that she wondered whether some- one — like Walt — could be strongly attracted to two people at the same time.

"My problem is just the opposite of yours, Melon," Nancy said. "I don't know exactly who Mr. Wonderful would be for me." Then she turned to Olivia. "See how lucky you are?"

"Guess so," Olivia muttered, averting her eyes.

Olivia had difficulty pretending, and her friends knew something was wrong. Nancy and Mary Ellen were too tactful to ask any direct questions, but they were sure there was a lot she wasn't tell- ing.

"Ready to leave now?" Mary Ellen asked.

"I'm ready," Olivia answered.

"Let's go then," Nancy said.

Mary Ellen led the way and looked down each row of lockers as they headed for the exit. "I think we're the last to leave," she remarked.

They had come to the last row, and Nancy whispered, "Except for the Sphinx." She tilted her head toward Samantha, who was sitting half- dressed on the bench in front of her locker and seemed to be staring into space.

The girls paid no attention to her, and con- tinued walking and chatting. "I wonder if Saman- tha will make the squad," Mary Ellen said.

"If the judges want a silent beauty, she'll make it," Nancy commented. "Actually, I think she's a little uptight in her performance."

"Who do you think will be chosen?" Mary Ellen asked.

"Jessica, for sure," Nancy replied. "She's got it all — looks, talent, everything."

"She sure does," Olivia said, and restrained herself from saying, Looks, talent . . . and probably Walt.

They were halfway down the hall when they saw Angie rushing out of the yearbook office.

"What did you forget?" Mary Ellen asked.

"Can't find my watch — think I left it in the locker room. I was in such a hurry . . ." she explained as she sped past them.

"Love doesn't care about time," Nancy called after her, and they all laughed, Angie most of all.

Angie ran to her locker. She was so preoccupied with retrieving her watch that she didn't notice anyone else was there. She was just about to open the safety lock when she heard a muffled sob. She froze, and strained to listen harder, wanting to make sure she wasn't imagining things. The sound became more distinct, and Angie knew for sure that someone was crying. She followed the sound, and then saw a girl hunched over on a bench.

Angie cleared her throat, not wanting to alarm whoever it was. She knew the distraught person thought she was alone, and maybe didn't want anyone invading her privacy. But Angie couldn't resist her impulse to help. She walked softly toward the girl, and then said with surprise, "Samantha, it's you!"

Samantha raised her head, her face streaked with tears, and sobbed even louder. Angie couldn't believe what she was seeing: the cool, collected Samantha, dissolved in tears. She instinctively sat down beside Samantha, put her arm around her shoulder, and asked gently, "What's happened? Were you hurt?"

Samantha, still unable to speak, nodded her head.

"Where?" Angie looked her over, trying to discern what part of her body had been injured.

Still Samantha said nothing.

"Wait," Angie said, "I'll get you some paper towels and we can mop up. Don't go away."

Angie went to the sink, moistened a paper towel, and brought it back along with a handful of dry ones. She gave them to Samantha, who dabbed her eyes and cheeks, and then blotted her face dry. Slowly Samantha regained her composure, the sobbing subsided, and she was able to mumble, "Thank you."

"Now tell me what you did to yourself," Angie persisted, once again examining Samantha's limbs for a sign of injury. "I don't see anything wrong."

"It's not physical. It's . . . it's something else."

Angie knew immediately that "it" must have to do with hurt feelings. She guessed that Samantha, who had so many male pursuers, was probably having boy trouble.

"There are so many guys that go for you," Angie assured her, "you shouldn't get thrown by one."

"Huh?" Samantha looked puzzled.

"What I mean is, every girl I know has had a similar experience. At least once in a lifetime. . . ."

Samantha smiled sadly. "That's not what happened, Angie. *That* I could handle."

"This is like twenty questions. It's not physical, and it's not anything to do with boys. I don't want to pry, so don't answer if you don't want to, but it must have something to do with your family."

Samantha shook her head. "I don't feel you're prying. In fact, you're being so nice to me. You're the first girl that's spoken to me since . . . since. . . ." Her lower lip started to tremble and she couldn't go on.

Angie was stunned to realize that Samantha was trying to tell her that she was having problems with girls. It was difficult for her to comprehend, because Angie made friends so easily. "I'm not sure I understand, Samantha."

Samantha took a deep breath, and tried to explain. "I've felt so out of it with all the girls, and today it really got to me. Everybody's talking about the cheerleading party, and I think I'm the only one who's not invited. One of the reasons I wanted to go out for the squad was to make friends, and now I'm worse off than ever."

"But Samantha," Angie said, "you're — you never talk to anyone. I see you're always surrounded by boys, but you act so . . . so superior."

"I don't feel that way. I just think none of the girls likes me, and that makes me clam up." She looked miserable.

"Just because you're gorgeous and have a zillion guys." Angie was kidding, trying to cheer her up, but then she realized that what she'd said was true. Samantha *was* gorgeous and she *did* have a zillion guys. "That's no reason not to talk to people!"

"I'm shy," she said simply.

It was hard for Angie to believe that anyone who looked like Samantha could be shy. Then she figured that maybe that was the reason — that Samantha had been "ooohhed" and "aaahhed" over so much as a little girl that she never had to say anything. Her looks said it all!

"Look," Angie said, "I think everyone has the wrong impression of you. I have to admit I did, too. But now that I understand you better . . . well, I think things can change."

"What do you mean?"

"If you give me permission, I'll explain everything to Nancy. She's really terrific, and once she understands how you feel . . . well, I know you'll be invited to the party."

Samantha didn't say anything, and her eyes misted again.

"You *do* want to go to the party, don't you?" Angie said finally.

"More than anything."

"Then what's wrong, Samantha?"

"I just feel so foolish . . . falling apart like this, and dumping my problems on you, and — "

"That's ridiculous. Actually, I've learned a lot from you."

"I can't believe that. What could you possibly have learned from me?"

"That things aren't always what they seem . . . and it's a mistake to make snap judgments."

"You know something, Angie, I've watched you perform and I think you have such a natural talent for cheerleading. But more than that, you've got a real talent for friendship."

72

"Thanks for saying that, Samantha. After today, I believe you do, too."

Nancy couldn't have been more surprised when she learned from Angie that Samantha was devastated by not being invited to her party. She remembered all too well how she had felt left out when she first came to Tarenton High, and how much it meant to her to make friends. Nancy knew enough about psychology to realize that Samantha's coolness was a form of self-protection. When Angie told her that Samantha was actually in tears, Nancy didn't wait to send her an invitation. She called her on the phone that night.

When a boy answered, Nancy assumed he was Samantha's younger brother. She laughed out loud when she heard him yell, "Sam, it's for you. It's a girl!" Obviously that was a switch, and it confirmed in Nancy's mind that Samantha was probably starved for friendship.

"I want you to come to the cheerleading party at my house next Saturday," Nancy said. There was no point in apologizing for not inviting her sooner, or pretending the invitation had gotten lost in the mail.

"I'd love to," Samantha said. Nancy was surprised at how elated she sounded.

After Nancy told her the details of where and when, they got into a discussion about how Tarenton High was different from their previous schools. Nancy said that it had been really tough for her to enter Tarenton High as a junior.

"Me, too," Samantha said. "I'd gone to my other school since kindergarten."

Soon they were chatting like old friends, and for the first time since cheerleading practices started, Samantha was looking forward to going to school the next day. She'd been embarrassed about breaking down in front of Angie, but now she believed it was the best thing that could have happened.

CHAPTER

9

Peter Rayman stared at his image in the three-way mirror over the bathroom sink and wondered whether he should get a haircut before the party. Most girls liked boys with hair on the long side, but he didn't think the shaggy look suited him. Not the way it did Sean Dubrow, who seemed to be every girl's dream. Sean was so good-looking, so at ease and confident — especially with girls. He attracted them easily.

Peter didn't like dwelling on the difference between he and Sean, but he couldn't help it. They were the exact opposites, even down to their size and coloring. Sean was over six feet tall, dark-haired, handsome, and muscular; Peter was on the short side, had sandy-colored hair, and a skinny, wiry build. Their attitudes and personalities were different, too: Sean was irreverent and devil-may-care, while Peter was respectful and serious.

Sure, they had a few things in common — they were both only children living in single-parent homes. But there the similarity ended, for Sean lived with his father, Mark, and Peter lived with his mother.

Peter would never forget meeting Mr. Dubrow on Parents' Day at Tarenton High at the beginning of the year. He was an adult edition of Sean who came on just as strong. Peter thought of him as a super-salesman type, and wasn't surprised to learn that he *was* a salesman for Tarenton Fabricators. The story was that Sean's mother had died when Sean was quite young. Sean never mentioned her, but he frequently bragged about he and his father living together as bachelors.

Fran Rayman, Peter's mother, had been working full-time in the administration office of Haven Lake Medical Center for five years, ever since her divorce. Peter's father, Jim, had immediately remarried and moved to California, and Peter had very little contact with him. Although he loved his mother, it was a painful situation for Peter, who missed his father terribly. Peter also harbored some resentment toward him, and blamed him for his feelings of inadequacy around girls. If he had a father to advise him, the way Sean did, maybe things would be different.

Peter brushed his hair and decided to forget the haircut. The last time he'd gone to the barber he'd been scalped, and he didn't want to risk that again. It had made him very self-conscious, and Sean's joke when they happened to be in study hall together — "I see you got your ears lowered" — didn't help.

Fran didn't get home until six, so Peter was responsible for getting things ready for supper. They'd worked out a system where Fran prepared a number of dishes over the weekend that she froze. Then all that was necessary was to heat them in the microwave oven and fix a soup or salad during the week. Peter had performed this routine since he was eleven years old, and didn't think too much about it. He tried not to let it bother him that Sean invariably mentioned some swinging restaurant he and his father had gone to — even on school nights!

Fran was a calm, intelligent woman who was aware of her inclination to protect her son and depend on him for companionship. Even though she worked long hours and had quite a few friends, she had to curb her desire to become too involved in Peter's personal life. He was an excellent student and sang in the chorus, which pleased Fran enormously, but she believed he needed something else.

Fran knew that Peter was exceptionally well-coordinated. She had taken him ice-skating, a sport she loved, when he was four years old. He adapted to it so quickly that he soon surpassed his mother in his ability to spin and glide on the ice, and amazed everyone in sight. The problem was, there wasn't an ice-skating club at school, and Fran thought Peter's athletic talent wasn't being tapped.

She knew Peter didn't like it when she made suggestions about what he should do. But then she happened to read in the Tarenton High newspaper, which Peter brought home, a small box at the bottom of the sports page:

PUT A LITTLE RAH-RAH IN YOUR LIFE!
TRY OUT FOR CHEERLEADING!
NO EXPERIENCE NECESSARY
TUESDAY 3:45 — GYM

"I'll bet that's fun," Fran said, as she glanced at the paper while waiting for the coffee to finish perking for breakfast.

"What are you talking about?" Peter asked.

"Cheerleading. I bet you'd be terrific at it."

"Maybe."

"Mrs. Poletti cut my hair last week, and she was telling me all about it. Angie loves it."

"That's nice."

"She says cheerleading has been one of her happiest experiences at Tarenton. Says it's really challenging — it requires enormous skill."

"You mean I should try out for the squad?"

"I thought I was being subtle," Fran said, trying to keep things light.

Peter smiled. He knew his mother didn't mean to interfere. He listened.

"Anyway, how about it?" Fran persisted.

Peter didn't show that he was annoyed even when his mother tried to impose her views on him. But inside he was pretty irritated.

He took the coffeepot off the stove, filled two mugs, carried them to the kitchen table, sat down opposite Fran, and idly stirred some sugar into his cup. It had occurred to him, too, that he would have liked to have participated in a sport.

He wasn't all that competitive, and being part of a squad that required mutual support suited his personality. The tryouts might be an ordeal, but Peter had confidence in his athletic prowess. If he didn't make the squad, well . . . he'd worry about that later.

"I think it's a good idea, Mom," Peter said simply. "I'm going to do it."

"Wonderful!" Fran exclaimed. "If it's half as much fun as Angie says, you'll even love practicing for the tryouts."

"That remains to be seen, but I think it's worth this risk."

The first few weeks of practice had been fun in ways Peter never had dreamed possible. Even though he didn't have the brute strength that Sean exhibited, he felt completely at ease executing the technical maneuvers. And there had been fringe benefits that he hadn't anticipated — mainly getting to see Hope. Actually, they had three classes together, but they never got close enough to speak.

Peter took a casserole out of the freezer, unwrapped the foil, leaned against the refrigerator, and daydreamed about Hope. He felt so inexperienced with girls, and there was no one he could talk to. He'd feel like a complete nerd if he asked a friend about how to attract a girl. Still, he could dream about her . . . and maybe soon he'd find an excuse to do more than that. Also, he couldn't wait for the cheerleading party. Maybe then something would happen.

Meanwhile, there was tomorrow to look forward to. Ardith had said something at the last practice about the boys being sure to get eight hours' sleep and taking an extra dose of vitamins, because at the next session they were going to work on the proper way to lift the girls. Just thinking about clasping Hope around the waist and raising her into the air made Peter flush. If only he could gather his courage and ask her during the warm-ups to be his partner. . . .

He wondered what Sean would say: Hey, babe, since you're the lightest one here, how about you and me showing them how it's done? or I've looked over the field, and I like your style — also your weight. No point in me straining a muscle. . . . Both of those approaches were gross, Peter thought, but Sean was capable of getting away with them.

Peter thought, maybe I should just go up to her and say point blank, Do you want to practice lifts with me? That would be simple enough, but what if she said no? Then what would I do? If she rejects me, does that mean we're finished? But how can something be finished if it hasn't even started?

Peter was so absorbed in his thoughts that he didn't hear his mother pull the Toyota into the driveway. He was startled to see her standing at the kitchen door, and hoped he hadn't spoken out loud. If he had, Fran had the good grace not to mention it.

"Hi, Pete," she said. "I see you got out the tuna casserole."

"What?" Peter was momentarily disoriented,

and wasn't sure what she was talking about.

"The tuna casserole. That object you're holding in your hand."

"Oh, this," he said, looking at the dish as though it were a foreign object that had mysteriously found its way into his grasp.

Fran nodded her head. "You also seem to be glued to the fridge. Are you able to move?"

"Oh, sure, Mom. I was just thinking about something."

"I'm going to wash up, so you get things started."

"You want me to get things started, right?"

Fran shook her head and turned to leave the room. She murmured to herself, loud enough for Peter to hear, "If I didn't know you better, I'd say you were falling in love."

Peter had trouble getting through classes the next day. It didn't help that in history he sat in his assigned seat in the back of the room where he had a perfect view of the back of Hope's head. She was in the second row and therefore totally unaware that she was being scrutinized. He memorized every detail of her hair and decided he'd never seen anything so lustrous and gleaming.

He was only half listening to Mr. Kramer, who sprinkled his lectures with questions, until Hope was called on. Then Peter gave him his full attention and found himself breathing faster.

"Hope," Mr. Kramer asked, "what three countries comprised the Axis powers during World War II?"

"Japan, Germany, and . . . and. . . ." Hope named two of the countries without a moment's hesitation, but then she floundered.

"That's right so far," Mr. Kramer encouraged her. "What's the third?"

Another moment of silence, finally broken by Peter, who was identifying so much with Hope that he involuntarily cried out, "Italy!"

Everyone in the class, including Hope, laughed and turned to stare at the source of their amusement.

Mr. Kramer, who was known for his sarcastic sense of humor, said dryly, "Peter Rayman, I didn't know your name was Hope Chang."

That made the class laugh even louder, and Peter turned a bright shade of pink. Then he slid down in his chair as far as he possibly could without winding up on the floor. He was so mortified, he wasn't sure how he could get through the rest of the period. It didn't help that a few minutes later, after Mr. Kramer lectured on the territorial ambitions of the Axis powers, he directed a question to Peter.

"Peter, what was Hitler's attitude toward the Versailles Treaty?"

"He didn't like it."

"That happens to be the correct answer, but would you mind elaborating?"

Peter dreaded being the center of attention, especially after making such a fool of himself. But he knew matters could only get worse if he refused, so he swallowed hard and plunged in.

"The Versailles Treaty was the formal agreement that ended World War I. It stripped Germany of much of its land and did not allow for any militarization to take place in Germany. In other words, it was an attempt to make Germany a second-rate power."

"Not a bad answer," Mr. Kramer said approvingly.

This time everyone turned around and looked at Peter with admiration. And Hope smiled at him so sweetly that he thought he might melt.

If this is what falling in love is all about, Peter mused, I'm not sure I'll survive.

Peter wanted to be one of the first to arrive for cheerleading practice. He figured if he got there early, he could maneuver himself next to Hope for the warm-ups. Then, when the lifts began, it would be the most natural thing in the world for them to be partners.

He hurriedly changed into his shorts and T-shirt, and went into the gym. He was surprised to see that Tara and Sally were already there, and hadn't yet bothered to change clothes. They were still in their jeans. Tara, apparently, had just finished showing Sally some part of a routine, for Sally was saying, "Oh, Tara, I think you're right. This would be a terrific finale for my tryout. You're sweet to have shown it to me."

"Don't mention it. Seeing as I'm not using it, it's yours. Now let's get changed or we'll be late."

Peter sat down on the front row of the bleachers and watched them leave. His strategy was to wait for Hope, follow her with his eyes, and then somehow find himself next to her so that conversation was at least a possibility. He still wasn't sure how it might begin, but maybe by some miracle. . . .

At that moment, just as he was imagining an opening line, his plans were abruptly terminated. For there were Sean and Hope, drifting into the gym, talking nonstop. Upon closer inspection, Peter realized that Sean was doing all the talking. But so what! Peter had been one-upped by Sean, who must have carefully timed it so that he and Hope would bump into each other in the common hall that led from the locker rooms to the gym.

Peter was crestfallen. Of all the girls in Tarenton, why did Sean have to go for Hope? Maybe he was just playing games with her, the way he was reputed to do with a lot of girls. Or maybe after the incident in history class, where Peter inadvertently revealed his feelings for Hope, Sean thought it would be amusing to throw a monkey wrench into a budding romance. Or worst of all, maybe Hope sought out Sean. Peter tormented himself with that idea, which was promptly reinforced when he saw her reaction to something Sean had said. She still hadn't spoken, but she looked at Sean with those dark eyes. Peter steamed with jealousy.

"What's the matter, Pete?" a friendly voice asked. "You look like you're ready to explode."

Peter looked up and saw Carla Simpson looming over him. He tried to reply normally, "Oh, nothing, Carla. I was just daydreaming."

"More like nightmaring, from the look on your face. Anyhow, we're going to do lifts today. Are you feeling strong?"

84

"I could eat nails," Peter answered, a response that could be interpreted several different ways.

"That's good, because I thought maybe you would be my partner. We're about the same height."

It was true that they were approximately the same height, but Carla was at least fifteen pounds heavier. Peter was too polite to refuse her suggestion, but all he could muster was a simple, "Yes."

Carla was a pleasant girl, who was serious about losing weight. She was so honest and forthright about her problem that it was hard not to sympathize. She even admitted that trying out for cheerleading might help her achieve her weight-loss goal of twenty pounds.

Peter, who was so sensitive himself and would never deliberately hurt Carla's feelings, was afraid it would be hard to lift her. He unconsciously spread his fingers and gazed at his hands.

"Don't worry," Carla said, reading his mind. "This is just practice. When and if I make the squad, I'll be at least ten pounds lighter."

Peter wondered what good that would do him today, but he didn't tell her that. Instead, he lied and said, "I'm not worried."

"Let's find a space for warm-ups. The session is about to begin."

Peter resigned himself to his fate and stood up. He tried to will himself not to look at Sean and Hope, but he couldn't help passing them as he followed Carla. Hope was sitting cross-legged on the floor, wearing a lavender leotard that reminded Peter of a purple iris: delicate and lovely.

"Come on, Peter," Carla called.

"I'm on my way," Peter answered, and stumbled over Sean's leg which hadn't been extended until that second. Sean was in a crouched position, balancing himself on one leg while he stretched the other.

Peter managed not to fall, but he was sure Sean had invented that exercise for the sole purpose of tripping him. He was even more sure when Sean said, "Watch it, buddy. I'm trying something new."

Peter was so angry, he was speechless. All he could do was stand there and glare at Sean.

Hope looked at him worriedly and leaped gracefully to her feet. "Are you all right, Peter?" she asked.

They were the first words she'd ever spoken to him, and his head reeled. It took him a moment to regain his senses, and then he answered softly, "Now I am — now I'm definitely all right."

After that, Peter breezed through the exercises, and when it came time for the lifts, he felt imbued with the powers of Superman. He and Carla may have not been the best-suited couple on the floor, but at least they weren't making fools of themselves.

"You're even stronger than I thought," Carla complimented him after Peter raised her in the air.

"Let's say I was inspired," he said, grinning happily.

CHAPTER

When Mary Ellen arrived home after practice, her little sister Gemma was waiting for her at the door. She couldn't wait to give her the message.

"Mrs. Gunderson called three times," she said urgently, "and you're supposed to call her the minute you come in."

"I wonder what that's all about," Mary Ellen said, going into the small bedroom she shared with Gemma. She hung up her jacket in the closet and dumped her books on the floor.

"Maybe you're getting a raise," Gemma suggested. She idolized Mary Ellen, and assumed everyone else did as well.

"I only work at Marnie's part-time, and the owner of the shop isn't about to call me on the phone to tell me I'm getting a raise. Sometimes, Gemma, I wonder about your brains."

"It was just a thought. Anyhow, you better call her."

Mary Ellen went into the kitchen to use the phone. The other one was in her parents' bedroom, and unless she had a very private call to make, she didn't bother to go there. Since most of her friends had their own phone, this was just another reminder of what *she* didn't have.

One of the reasons she was so happy to work at Marnie's was because it gave her some extra spending money and allowed her to buy clothes at a discount. Also, she luxuriated in the opulence of the elegant store that catered to fashionable women. Someday, she fantasized as she dialed the number, she would be one of those women who didn't have to worry about how much anything cost.

The phone rang five times, and Mary Ellen figured that the shop might be closed since it was already past five. She was about to hang up, when someone picked up and said breathlessly, "Hello."

Mary Ellen immediately recognized the aristocratic voice of the owner, who looked exactly like she sounded — elegant and efficient. "Hello, Mrs. Gunderson."

"Thank goodness you called, Mary Ellen. The situation is desperate."

"What's happened?"

"The Women's Club asked me for a donation today for World Drought Relief, and I came up with a better idea. I suggested that Marnie's have a fashion show — the members of the club would drum up the potential buyers, and twenty-five percent of everything that was sold would be donated to the cause. They were thrilled with the idea, but now I have to arrange a show. I need you, Mary Ellen, and anyone else you think might be interested in modeling for the day." Mrs. Gunderson was pleading.

"When is it?" Mary Ellen asked.

"This Saturday, from two to four. You don't have to work that day. This is for a worthy cause."

"I'll do it," Mary Ellen said. "And I'll ask the girls on the cheerleading squad if they'd like to help out, too."

"That's a marvelous idea. I'm sure they're the model type."

"You don't have to worry about that." Mary Ellen took pride in the fact that she was captain of such an attractive group.

"There's hardly any time to rehearse, but if you tell me their exact measurements, I'll find the correct sizes. We'll be showing the summer line: sportswear, summer dresses, beach clothes. Do you think you could have the girls over to your house before Saturday and brief them on how to walk and turn?"

Mary Ellen hesitated. She hated having anyone visit her house. It was so tacky, in her opinion.

"Never mind, dear," Mrs. Gunderson said quickly, "we'll have a dry run on Saturday morning, try on the clothes, practice parading down the aisle. . . ."

"They're very fast learners," Mary Ellen assured her, relieved that she didn't have to explain her reluctance to invite the girls to her house.

"I'm sure of that. I just hope they will do it, even though I can't pay them. It *is* for charity. . . ."

"They're my friends," said Mary Ellen reassuringly. "I'm sure they will."

"Will you let me know this evening how many I can count on? You can call me at home."

"I'll do that, Mrs. Gunderson. I have your home number."

"I'm so excited about this, and I so appreciate your help, Mary Ellen."

"I'll call you later."

"Thank you, thank you, and good-bye for now."

As soon as Mary Ellen hung up, Gemma bombarded her with questions. The details elevated her opinion of Mary Ellen more than ever. "Just think, Melon, you'll be the leader of the models, just like you are of the cheerleaders. Can I go and watch Saturday?"

"I think that could be arranged, especially if you stop calling me that awful name."

"Sorry, it just slipped out. Now tell me more about what Mrs. G. said."

"Not until I make some calls, otherwise this thing will never happen."

Mary Ellen spent the next half hour calling her friends, telling them the predicament Mrs. Gunderson had gotten herself into, how she wanted to bail her out, and asking them if they would help. Both Nancy and Angie thought it would be fun. Only Olivia had some reservations.

"I'll have to see." Olivia sighed. "I'd love to, but. . . ." She didn't finish the sentence, but Mary

Ellen knew what she was trying to tell her.

"Don't worry. If your mother won't let you, then you can sit with Gemma and lead the applause. We'll need all the moral support we can get."

"Can't be any objections to that," Olivia said lamely. Then she asked, "Are you going to ask anyone else?"

"I don't plan to. I thought it would be kind of fun to make this an exclusive Varsity Squad show. See what you can do."

"I'll let you know." Olivia didn't sound too optimistic.

"Later," Mary Ellen said, and hung up.

After that she called Mrs. Gunderson, who was thrilled that she could count on three girls. "That's better than I expected," she said, "and you did say there might be a fourth."

"I should know tomorrow."

"I don't know what I'd do without you, Mary Ellen."

Mary Ellen felt an unexpected glow, knowing she had calmed down her usually unflappable boss. She was even willing to answer Gemma's exhaustive questions. And it flashed through her mind that someday she might have her own modeling agency.

Meanwhile, the minute Olivia got off the phone, she was grilled by her mother. "What was that all about?" Mrs. Evans inquired. Olivia had answered the phone in the living room, and her mother had made no pretense of not listening. She promptly came into the room, flopped down on the sofa, and took in every word.

"There's going to be a fashion show at Marnie's for World Drought Relief, and Mary Ellen asked me if I'd be one of the models with the girls from the squad."

"No, I don't like it, Olivia. I don't want my daughter parading around in front of a bunch of strangers."

"It's for a good cause. All the other girls are going to do it."

"What other girls?"

"Mary Ellen and Nancy and Angie."

"Those cheerleaders — I'm not surprised. Their main purpose in life is to show off their bodies. I can't believe their parents approve. And now this!"

"It's for charity, and we'll be showing the summer line."

"That's even worse, Olivia. You'll probably be asked to model those new bathing suits. Seems the less material the manufacturers use, the more they think they can charge. I refuse to allow you to be a clothes horse. And that's final!"

Olivia could see her mother was adamant, and that there was no more point in arguing. She felt tired and defeated.

"Okay, Mother, you win." Olivia stood up, mumbling that she had to study for a math test. She went into her room, closed the door, and leaned against it. She told herself it was just a dumb fashion show, but tears welled up in her eyes, and she knew it was more than that. Once again the girls on the squad were doing something without her, and she was the outsider. It wasn't their fault, but it was still a fact of life.

She'd be an onlooker and they'd be having all the fun.

Maybe I shouldn't bother to go, she thought. I could pretend I have a dentist appointment. But that would be such an obvious lie, the girls would see right through it. Might as well tell them the truth: My mother won't let me!

Olivia suddenly felt weak and dizzy, and she stumbled towards her bed and fell onto it. Then she gave in to her tears and for the next five minutes cried her heart out. She'd always been a fighter, but lately she was caving in to her emotions. Was it possible, she wondered, for a sixteen-year-old girl to be suffering from burnout?

Saturday morning Mary Ellen, Angie, and Nancy arrived at Marnie's at nine o'clock, two hours before the store opened. They each carried sandals, as instructed. Elsie Gunderson, Tessie Hamburg, Marnie's ebullient seamstress, and Abby Bennett, Jessica's mother, who worked as a salesperson, were in the stock room. That wasn't the least bit surprising, but the girls were astounded to see Jessica there, looking through the clothes.

They exchanged hi's but Mary Ellen was particularly cool toward Jessica, whom she considered to be invading her territory. Mary Ellen softened a little when the "intruder" said, "I hope you don't mind that I've been brought in as a ringer. I know this was probably meant to be a show put on by the Varsity Squad, but — "

"I knew you girls would understand," Mrs. Gunderson promptly explained. "At the last minute I decided that four models would be better than three, and Mrs. Bennett suggested Jessica."

"That's okay," Angie said. Her generous spirit would never allow her to be petty, and she wanted to put everyone at ease.

"We understand," Nancy said, and Mary Ellen nodded her head.

"Now let me tell you what's happening," Mrs. Gunderson continued. "I've set up four racks of clothes — one for each of you. You can try everything on and make sure the sizes are right. The clothes are lined up in the order in which I want you to show them. You'll see that we'll start with shorts and tops, next bathing suits, then short summer dresses, and finally evening wear."

"Aren't we going to have music?" Nancy asked.

"Yes, indeed. Thanks to Jessica, she's arranged for Walt Manners to provide us with a cassette deck and tapes. His family, you know, does the local TV broadcast, and he's familiar with show business. He's going to be here any minute to help us synchronize the music with the modeling. I thought it was a marvelous idea of Jessica's to ask him."

Mary Ellen, Nancy, and Angie reacted to this piece of information with stony silence. It was a good idea, but what did this mean as far as Olivia was concerned? Was Jessica moving in on Walt?

"Is something wrong?" Jessica asked. She was truly bewildered.

"Not really," Angie said. "We're just surprised we didn't think of it first — right, girls?"

Nancy and Mary Ellen forced themselves to

laugh, taking their cue from Angie to not reveal what they were thinking.

"Who else did you invite, Jessica?" Mary Ellen asked, half kidding.

"Pres and Patrick," she replied guilelessly.

"What for?" Nancy asked.

"Oh, that was really my doing," Mrs. Bennett explained. "Else asked me who I could think of to arrange chairs and lay the runner, and I asked Jessica. She, in turn, asked Walt, who suggested Pres and Patrick because they have a moving truck, and could pick up the folding chairs from the rental company — saving us a lot of money — and also set them up."

At first Mary Ellen had been put at ease by Jessica's honesty about inviting Walt. But *this* was a little much. She wasn't quite sure why, because she didn't want a permanent relationship with Patrick or Pres, who she hadn't dated in ages — but she liked to be the one to call the shots. If anyone was going to ask Patrick and Pres to help out, it should have been her!

Angie saw that her friend was bristling, and in order to avoid a scene, she said, "Mrs. G., I think we should get started. We've got all these things to try on and some of them might not fit, and then. . . ."

"You're absolutely right, dear. Let's begin with the shorts and tops. Everyone change, and Mary Ellen will show us the proper modeling technique. The red velvet runner will separate two blocks of seats and lead to the raised platform in the window. Once there, you will climb the three steps — toe, heel, toe, heel, head high, arms loose but not flailing — pivot gracefully, and descend."

Mary Ellen prided herself on her professional attitude and refused to let her personal feelings affect her performance. After all, Jessica had arranged for three boys — not just Patrick — to help out. Besides, she didn't want to get too serious about him. Next year, if she did go to New York, she'd be on her own, without Patrick or anyone else to depend on. Maybe this was good practice for what it would be like.

She changed into a pair of electric-blue shorts, tucked in a matching striped shirt, and slipped into her huaraches. Her face was a little flushed and her hair slightly disheveled. She started to comb it, but Mrs. Gunderson took one look at her and cried, "Mary Ellen, don't change a thing. You look perfect! Those tendrils framing your face add just the right touch of casualness. Am I right, girls?"

They all agreed that she did look wonderful, and Jessica summed up her appearance. "You look like an ad for a Caribbean vacation." And Mrs. Bennett observed, "That outfit looks like it was custom-made."

It was difficult, with all the compliments, for Mary Ellen to stay in a bad mood, especially when Jessica was so complimentary. She thought that maybe she'd been imagining things. Jessica had been so open about everything, and she certainly wasn't vicious.

"Why is it when my hair is messed up, I look like I've been through an eggbeater, but when Mary Ellen's is messy, she's more glamorous than ever?" Angie asked wistfully.

That made everyone laugh, and soon they were all talking up a storm, trying on clothes, outdoing one another with praise.

"Hello there!" someone shouted from the main room. "The music man is here."

The girls were in various stages of undress, and hearing Walt's voice made them overreact. "Help!" "Don't come in!" "We'll be out in a minute."

"I'll take care of him," Mrs. Gunderson said, leaving the girls bustling and laughing.

Minutes later, Walt had made the connections so that the music was piped into the main room. He adjusted the sound and explained that he had tapes for every mood, from country western to hard rock.

"We'll settle for something romantic and melodious — new, but not too far out," Mrs. Gunderson suggested.

"Gotcha," Walt said, and dug out a tape from his carrying case that combined just the right ingredients.

Then Mary Ellen sashayed down the aisle, smiling at the imaginary audience, and gracefully negotiated the steps leading to the platform, twirled around to show her outfit from every vantage point, and retraced her steps. Everyone — Walt and Tessie most of all — bravoed her performance, and then the other girls tried to imitate her technique. There were a few false starts, but because of their natural athletic ability and grace, they caught on almost immediately.

Less than two hours later, they had mastered the correct walk, facial expression — pleasantly cool — and the order in which they were to appear. With a few minor adjustments to their clothes by the nimble-fingered Tessie, they were ready.

Mrs. Gunderson called a lunch break just as Pres and Patrick arrived with their moving van. The girls were feeling overly energetic, and in spite of Mrs. Gunderson's protestations that they should save themselves until the show, they insisted on helping unload the truck. With everyone pitching in, the room was set up in no time.

Mrs. Gunderson slipped a bill to Pres and insisted that the workers have a pizza on Marnie's.

"Please be back at one-thirty girls, and come in the back door. I don't want the customers seeing our stars before the main event."

"We can watch, can't we, Mrs. G.?" Pres asked.

"Well, I honestly thought this would be a 'For Women Only' show."

"Please," Walt pleaded, tilting his head in a hangdog look and holding his hands up like paws.

The staid Mrs. Gunderson crumpled over with laughter. "Oh, all right. I don't see why not," she conceded.

"I have my camera and I'll take some pictures," Patrick offered. "That'll make my presence official — and maybe I'll get them in the local paper."

"Great idea," Mrs. Bennett said. "That would give the Women's Club, World Drought Relief, and Marnie's some excellent publicity."

98

"I never thought of that," Mrs. Gunderson admitted. "But who could write it up?"

"I know who," Mary Ellen piped up. "Olivia."

"Is she coming?" Walt asked. It was hard to tell if he was surprised, alarmed, or just interested.

"Yes, she is," Mary Ellen answered. "And we all know she's a good writer."

"That would be wonderful," Mrs. Gunderson said. "Will you call and ask her?"

"Be glad to. . . . I'll do it right now."

Mary Ellen went into the back office and reappeared a few minutes later.

"She'd love to," Mary Ellen reported, and glanced at Walt to gauge his reaction. But Walt was bent over his cassette carrying case, struggling with the zipper, so there was no way to know what he was thinking.

"I'm starved!" Angie cried. "Let's get going before I faint."

"Follow me," Pres ordered, and marched toward the truck while Mrs. Gunderson, Mrs. Bennett, and Tessie looked on.

They started clambering into the van when Mary Ellen suddenly ran back toward the store. "Don't leave without me," she called. "I left my bag in the office."

Minutes later she emerged, bag in hand, and brushed by the onlookers just in time to hear Tessie say, "Such wonderful young people. So happy, so carefree."

Mary Ellen smiled a little cynically, shook her head, and thought, Tessie, you should only know.

CHAPTER

Olivia was delighted that she had been asked
to write up the show. Mary Ellen was rushing so
much that she hadn't had a chance to fill her in
on any of the details, but Olivia wasn't worried.
The school newspaper had published many of
her stories, so she felt she could wing it. Mary
Ellen did tell her to be there at a quarter to two,
to come in the back door, and that a seat would
be reserved for her.

The fact that she was involved rather than just
a spectator appealed to Olivia greatly. Although
she wasn't one of the models, she no longer felt
like a fifth wheel. Stuffing a spiral notebook and
half dozen ballpoint pens into her bag, her sense
of being left out had practically vanished.

It was a perfect spring day, which added to her
restored high spirits. Olivia gave herself plenty
of time so that she could stroll to Marnie's at a
leisurely pace. Her parents had left earlier to do

the marketing for the week, so no explanations about where she was going were required.

As Olivia walked along, she considered an appropriate opening sentence, knowing that was crucial in order to grab her readers. By the time she reached Marnie's, she'd considered and rejected a dozen possibilities, but was confident the show would inspire her.

Olivia went around to the back of the store, and since the door was open, walked right in. The place was bustling with activity, and for a few minutes no one even noticed her. The good feelings she had on the way over quickly faded. Who am I kidding? she asked herself. I'm not part of this group and probably never will be. She felt more isolated than ever as she listened to their conversations.

Angie had tied her hair back in a ponytail and was asking if anyone thought she should wear it that way when she modeled the sportswear. No one bothered to answer, and she said aloud, "I guess I won't."

Nancy was touching up her toenails with a bright red color. "Forgot all about going barefoot for the bathing-suit bit. Thank goodness I always carry my polish with me."

Mary Ellen was doing some mild stretching exercises. "Have to stay loose," she mumbled to no one in particular. "Relieves the tension."

Then Olivia noticed a fourth girl, whose back was to her. She was pressed close to the full-length mirror, applying blusher to her cheeks. It took Olivia less than sixty seconds to recognize the dark brown hair of Jessica. *Jessica!* Olivia caught her breath as she realized that Jessica was her replacement. Mrs. Gunderson had wanted four models, and since Olivia wasn't available, why not someone equally qualified?

Olivia was tempted to run away, and later come up with some excuse that would explain her not coming to the show. No one had spotted her, and she could just back out, sight unseen. She took a tentative step backward, but just at that moment Mary Ellen was coming up from a knee bend and saw her.

"Livvy!" she exclaimed. "You're here!"

All the girls shouted hello and continued their preparations. Then Mary Ellen introduced Olivia to Mrs. Gunderson, Mrs. Bennett, and Tessie.

"This is Olivia Evans, our star reporter."

"Oh, yes. I was so busy, I forgot about you, dear," Mrs. Gunderson said distractedly as she arranged Angie's collar. "I didn't put a reserve sign on a seat, so you'd better find one on the aisle before they're all taken."

Olivia thought she felt her heart fluttering. They forgot I was coming, she thought. Maybe if I'm lucky there won't be any seats left and I can escape.

"Come with me, Olivia," Mrs. Bennett said, before she had a chance to leave.

"I'll show you the best place to sit."

Relunctly, Olivia followed her into the salon, which was just beginning to fill up. There were still plenty of seats and Mrs. Bennett pointed to one on the aisle toward the back.

"You'll get the best perspective there," she advised.

"Thank you, Mrs. Bennett." Olivia didn't want to sound unappreciative. Olivia sat down and tried to ignore the discomfort in her chest, busily poking in her bag for her pad and pen, and told herself she was being ridiculous. Just because Jessica had replaced her was no reason to be so upset. If it had been anyone else — Samantha, Carla, or that bossy Holly — she wouldn't have been the least bit disturbed.

She had almost succeeded in calming down when Gemma bounded over to her. "Okay if I sit here? My sister said I could."

"Sure," Olivia answered. Olivia knew Gemma was a chatterbox, and she started taking notes so Gemma would get the idea that she was there for a purpose.

"Melon told me you were going to write this up and maybe get it published in the *Tarenton Lighter*. That would be super, especially if you got a byline. And Patrick's going to take pictures, so this — "

"Patrick's coming? I was sure this was strictly a fashion show for women."

"Well, it is, except the boys are helping out and I guess this is their reward."

"The boys? What boys?"

"The boys on the Varsity Squad, except for Patrick, but he and Pres had the truck and they picked up the chairs and stuff, and Walt is doing the music."

"Walt is doing the music?" Olivia repeated. She was stunned, and had trouble taking in all this information. No one had told her anything, not even Walt. She remembered telling him a week ago that she wouldn't be allowed to model, and all he'd said at the time was, "That's too bad."

Gemma, unaware of how Olivia was being affected, went right on talking. "You see, Jessica was called in at the last minute, and then I think it was her idea to get the boys to help out. Everyone thought it was a super idea, and you can see that it's worked out fine."

"I might have guessed," Olivia murmured.

"Guessed what?" Gemma asked.

Olivia didn't have to answer, because Walt, Patrick, and Pres were just making their entrance. Gemma exclaimed, "Here they are!"

If the boys had tried to make an inconspicuous entrance, it was too late now. There were a few raised eyebrows and some rather surprised looks among the women in the audience, but the boys ignored them.

Patrick had three cameras slung around his neck to explain his presence. He positioned himself near the platform while Pres found a front seat on the side — and Walt headed for the music equipment which he had set up in a back corner of the room. He strode down the aisle purposefully, and would have passed right by Olivia — was it by accident or design? — if Gemma hadn't shouted, "Hi, Walt. Where've you been? You're supposed to do the music."

Walt stopped short and chuckled. "I knew they wouldn't start the show without me."

He was about to continue walking when he noticed Olivia, who was scribbling away as if her life depended on it.

"Olivia, aren't you going to say hello?" he asked.

She looked up somberly and managed to say, "Hi."

"That's better," he said, and continued walking.

Olivia was ready to kill, and she wasn't sure why. Walt was being civil, so why couldn't she respond normally? An inner voice answered, Because he's here because of Jessica, not me. It's *her* he's come to see.

The music started playing softly, and the audience quieted down. Then Mrs. Gunderson, who had changed into an off-white linen suit, strode down the runner and climbed the steps, proving that she had never lost her modeling ability. In mellifluous tones, she thanked everyone for coming, told them how grateful Marnie's was to be able to make a contribution to such a worthy cause, and hoped everyone would enjoy the show.

"This is our summer line, and the clothes speak for themselves. Without further ado, let us begin." Mrs. Gunderson walked down the red runner, nodded to Walt to increase the volume, and disappeared into the back room where the girls were nervously waiting.

There was a ripple of applause as Mary Ellen glided down the aisle. It was hard to believe that she hadn't been modeling all her life. The audience buzzed their approval: "Isn't she adorable!" "I think we should buy it for our daughters." "I'd buy it for myself if I were thinner."

When Mary Ellen finished her turn, the applause increased and the girls were encouraged by the response. Angie, wearing warm green shorts and a polka-dotted shirt, and Nancy, in pale pink, performed without a flaw.

Olivia wrote careful descriptions of the clothes and the audience's reaction. She tried to concentrate on her assignment and not worry about Walt. He was a number of rows behind her, so fortunately she wasn't distracted by him. Then it was Jessica's turn, and it took Olivia all the will power she could muster not to look at Walt looking at *her*.

Jessica was wearing an outfit in an unusual shade of apricot that Olivia could only describe as sensational. It was enhanced by her extraordinary coloring, and Olivia didn't think that it was her imagination that the audience was impressed by it, too. As Jessica floated down the aisle, Olivia heard one woman say, "Breathtaking," another, "She looks like a porcelain doll," and a third, "Where did they find these girls? Each one is prettier than the next."

Olivia knew that a good reporter should be objective, and it would have been very unfair to play down Jessica's role. But she couldn't help thinking that *she* should have been the one wearing the apricot outfit, receiving the praise of the crowd, showing off for Walt. Life isn't fair, she thought, and forced herself to continue jotting down a description of how the fourth model moved with the delicacy of a doe.

Jessica had approached the platform and was moving up the steps in one graceful motion when she tripped. Her fall was so unexpected that the audience gasped. But before anyone made a move to help her, she had bounced to her feet. Then, as though Jessica wanted to assure everyone that no damage had been done, she twirled around a few times. Backstage, the other girls couldn't believe that *Jessica* was stealing the show.

The applause was thunderous and Jessica graciously bowed. Then she went down the steps and finished her turn as though nothing unusual had happened. Olivia knew this might well be the highlight of the show, and there was no way she could not play it up in her article. She, along with everyone else, had to admire anyone who was so poised and professional. But why, of all the people in the world, did it have to be Jessica who would steal the show?

"Wasn't she amazing?" Gemma asked. "I don't know anyone else who could have recovered so fast from a fall. I'm beginning to think Jessica can do anything!"

"I'm afraid you're right," Olivia muttered.

Gemma gave her a funny look, and was about to say something, but fortunately the bathing-suit segment was beginning. Mary Ellen appeared in a shocking pink one-piece suit, and Gemma was too excited to ask Olivia any more questions.

The rest of the show ran smoothly, and the finale, with the four girls in charming pastel evening dresses standing on the platform and holding hands, received a standing ovation.

Mrs. Gunderson appeared again and said, "I hope you've enjoyed this afternoon as much as I have, and I thank you all for coming."

Then a distinguished-looking, slim, silver-haired woman stood up and all eyes turned to her.

"As president of the Women's Club, I want to thank Mrs. Gunderson, Marnie's staff, and these extraordinary young women who put on this fabulous display. In order to show our appreciation, I hope each of you will make a purchase or a contribution to World Drought Relief."

This was received with polite applause, and soon everyone was milling around, talking to the girls, asking to see the clothes. The place was a beehive of activity. Gemma had jumped up from her seat and was running over to see Mary Ellen; Patrick was still clicking away, this time focusing on the customers; Pres and Walt were talking to Nancy and Jessica.

Olivia couldn't wait to get away, and now she had a legitimate excuse. If Mrs. Gunderson was serious about having a newspaper article on the show, it should appear immediately, she told herself. She picked up her bag and threaded her way through the crowd toward the back room where she could leave without being noticed.

Mrs. Bennett was rearranging some of the clothes the girls had worn, and saw Olivia out of the corner of her eye.

"Where you going?" she asked.

"Have to type up my article," Olivia said.

"Can't you stay a little while? It should be interesting to see how many sales we make after all this."

"I really have to work on this, Mrs. Bennett, so I can give it to Mrs. Gunderson tomorrow."

"Jessica told me the girls on the squad were

dedicated," Mrs. Bennett said, smiling. "Now I know what she meant!"

Olivia bit her lip, so that she wouldn't say aloud what she was thinking: That Jessica knows everything.

CHAPTER

Olivia had been working on her notes for more than two hours. She was her own most severe critic, but *she* even had to admit the article was shaping up nicely. If nothing else, Olivia was determined to live up to her reputation as a reliable reporter.

For the first time in months, Olivia did not have plans with Walt on a Saturday night. If he hadn't told her weeks ago that he had to go to his grandmother's birthday party, she might have been suspicious. She hadn't made any other plans, and now she was feeling a little sorry for herself.

It was almost six o'clock when the telephone rang. Her mother answered and shouted to Olivia that it was for her.

Olivia couldn't imagine who would be calling at this hour on a Saturday night — no one seemed to care that she had left Marnie's so early — and she was surprised to hear Patrick's voice.

"Why the disappearing act?" he asked, without bothering to say hello.

"I wanted to work on the article. If Mrs. Gunderson is serious about it, I should get it to her tomorrow."

"That's exactly why I'm calling. I'm developing my film right now, and I thought maybe we should get together and coordinate."

"I figured you'd be celebrating with the models all night."

"That, too," he said, laughing. "I mean they're here now to keep me company while I slave away for the cause."

"You, alone with four girls?" Olivia teased.

"Not exactly. I have lots of protection. Pres is here, and Angie invited Chris, of course, and Sean — he's like a bird dog when it comes to sniffing out where the action is — and Nancy's waiting for Eric. Mary Ellen and Jessica are coming, too. And soon you'll be here, with the article."

"Is that why you're inviting me?" Olivia was only half kidding.

"Stop being paranoid, Olivia. You belong here. Someone will pick you up in fifteen minutes."

"Okay. . . ." Olivia said hesitantly. She'd gotten so dependent on being paired with Walt that it wasn't easy for her to think of herself as going anywhere without him. But now . . . well, maybe she should branch out. "I'd like that, Patrick."

Olivia pulled the final page she'd been working on out of the typewriter and put it with the others in a manila envelope. She could do the editing at Patrick's house. Even if that was the only reason he asked her over, it was better than being at home on a Saturday night.

She changed into red stirrup pants and a white cotton sweater that happened to be Walt's favorite. No point in not looking good just because he wasn't going to be there. In fact, just the opposite. . . .

"Where are you going?" Mrs. Evans stood at the threshold of Olivia's bedroom door.

"I'm getting picked up in a few minutes. Going to Patrick's for a get-together."

"I thought you were staying home tonight."

"I thought so, too, Mother, but something's come up."

"Do you mind letting me in on it?"

Olivia liked to avoid confrontations with her mother, but she found it impossible to tell her an outright lie.

"I wrote up the fashion show at Marnie's today, and Patrick took some pictures, and we want to coordinate the whole thing for a feature story for the paper."

"Your father and I were expecting you to have dinner with us for once."

"Mother, it's Saturday night and before I didn't have plans, but now I do."

"Well, I don't know. You've been looking a little peaked lately — like you're doing too much."

Olivia geared herself up for an argument, but just as she was about to explode, she noticed her father standing behind his wife. He must have been listening to the whole conversation, because he said mildly, "It's not every day that you get your name in the paper."

Mrs. Evans turned to look at her husband and asked sharply, "What are you talking about?"

"I think Olivia will get a byline, and that's very important when it comes to getting into college."

Olivia was touched by her father's feeble attempt to persuade her mother that she should be allowed to leave, and she was amazed that it worked.

"Then you might as well go," Mrs. Evans said.

When her parents had left, Olivia was pleased with her small victory. She would have defied her mother and gone anyway, but her father's comment made things a lot easier.

She put on some lip gloss, ran a comb through her hair, slipped into low-cut boots, and was ready to leave when she heard a horn beeping outside. She peered out the window and saw an unfamiliar red Pontiac Fiero. Then a tall, muscular figure walked around to the passenger side, and Olivia recognized Sean.

Olivia was mildly surprised that Pres or Patrick hadn't picked her up, but she was in the mood for adventure. It would be fun to get to know somebody new — someone who wasn't graduating, and someone who was incredibly good-looking as well. Olivia was lighthearted as she flew down the stairs and waved good-bye to her parents, who were sitting down at the dining room table.

"Have fun," her father said.

"Don't get home too late," her mother called after her.

Sean held the passenger door open, beamed his toothpaste-smile at her, and said, "I like women who are on time. You already get points with me."

Olivia laughed a little nervously as she climbed into the car. "It's nice of you to pick me up."

"You're my assignment and, I must say, a very pretty one." Sean slammed the door shut, went around to the driver's side, and slid into the bucket seat. Then he gunned the motor, and sped off at an unnecessarily fast clip.

"I'm your *assignment*?" Olivia tightened her seat belt.

"Well, it seems everyone is linked up with someone, so I was the chosen one. I consider it a privilege. . . . I've had my eye on you at cheerleading practice, and you're fantastic. You're one of the reasons I hope to make the Varsity Squad . . . so I can get to know you better."

Olivia was flattered and a little wary at the same time. Less than an hour ago she'd been suffering from the Saturday Night Blues, and now she was being bestowed with compliments by a ruggedly handsome guy.

"There's no guarantee I'll be on the squad," she said simply. "Cheerleading is a lot of fun, but it's hard work, too."

"I won't mind the work if you're there to share it with me."

Olivia looked at him quizzically, but said nothing. Sean continued talking. "I know you and Walt have a thing going, but he won't be in school next year. And besides. . . ." He palmed the wheel around a curve and didn't finish his sentence.

"Besides what?" Olivia was sure he was going to mention something about Walt and Jessica. Painful as that would be, she had to know.

"Besides . . . nothing." Sean eyed Olivia out of the corner of his eye, waiting for her reaction. But Olivia was too reserved to press him.

"Hey, there's Patrick's house!" Olivia exclaimed as Sean sped past it, and then slammed on the brakes in front of an empty lot half a block away.

"Almost missed it," he sighed. "Talking to you makes my mind wander. Maybe if you gave me a kiss, I'd feel better." Sean hadn't bothered to put on a seat belt, but he reached over to release Olivia's.

"Sean, we're supposed to go to Patrick's so I can show him my story. He's waiting for us."

"I heard you were a worrywart, Olivia. There'll still be plenty of time for you and Patrick to collaborate. Let's do a little collaboration ourselves."

He put his arm around her and pulled her toward him.

"Sean, look, I don't know you at all," she protested.

"Now you will," he whispered, tilting her chin and pressing his mouth against hers.

Olivia hadn't kissed many boys, except for Walt, but she could tell Sean was experienced, and she couldn't help succumbing to his expertise. He started out slowly, gently, and then increased the pressure of his lips while at the same time managing to move his hand around her back in order to hold her close.

Olivia was thrilled and confused at the same

time. It flashed through her mind that she was being disloyal to Walt, but Walt hadn't been very attentive lately. Who knows what he and Jessica might have done without her knowing it? Almost defiantly, she kissed Sean back, and he muttered something about, "These stupid bucket seats are a menace, but we can always — "

"No!" Olivia shouted, and pulled away. "We can't always *anything*, and I think we should go in now."

"Okay, okay. I thought you were having a good time."

"I was . . . I mean it was all right, but — "

"No explanations necessary. We can continue this later . . . if you like." Sean released her, looked at his image in the rearview mirror, smoothed his hair with his fingers, and opened the door.

Sean was so cool that Olivia was more flustered than ever. If he'd given her an argument, forced her physically, she could have really gotten mad. Instead, he was being the perfect gentleman.

"Patrick's waiting for the article," she muttered, feeling foolish.

"I know he is. That's why we're here, remember?"

Olivia wasn't sure if he was making fun of her or not. "For a while there I almost forgot," she mumbled. Another dumb remark, she thought, but it didn't bother Sean. He helped her out of the car, took her hand, and together they walked toward Patrick's house.

"You're not only pretty, but interesting," Sean

remarked, as they waited for someone to answer the doorbell.

At that moment, Patrick thrust open the door. "Where've you guys been?" he asked. "Did you take the scenic route?"

"Olivia kept me waiting," Sean lied.

"A likely story," Patrick said chuckling.

Olivia wasn't sure if she appreciated Sean's explanation or not, but it was better than him bragging about their encounter in the Mazda. Not that anything had really happened, but it was the kind of thing that might get back to Walt . . . or maybe *should*.

"Help yourself to some food in the kitchen, Sean. And Livvy, come with me to the darkroom. I have someting to show you."

"Don't stay too long, or I'll get lonesome," Sean said. "Remember, Patrick, she's my assignment tonight."

Patrick had developed several rolls of film and printed contact sheets, which he showed to Olivia. Together they selected the ones that best described the four segments of the show and also dovetailed with Olivia's article. Olivia insisted on making editorial revisions, until Patrick reminded her that there were copy editors on the paper who would be out of a job if every writer were so meticulous.

"You're right," she said laughing, and put down her pencil. "Let's hear what the critics have to say."

Peter led the way into the living room, turned down the volume on the stereo, and asked everyone to be serious for a minute. Then, against Olivia's protestations, he insisted on reading the article aloud. It began, "The fashion show Saturday afternoon at Marnie's, for the benefit of World Drought Relief, was streamlined, stylish, and sensational." It went on to describe the ambience, the clothes, and the models.

When Patrick finished reading, there was a loud buzz of approval and Olivia glowed with embarrassment and pride.

"No suggestions?" she asked, and looked around at the attentive listeners.

Everyone shook their heads, indicating they were satisfied, and Sean said vigorously, "It's perfect."

"Next question — how do we get it to Mrs. Gunderson?" Patrick inquired.

"That's easy," Jessica piped up. "My mother is seeing her tomorrow to go over some paper work. There were so many sales today that they have to work Sunday to catch up."

"Jessica, you're a lifesaver," Patrick exclaimed.

"No problem," Jessica said. "I'll take the story and the pictures home with me tonight, and Mrs. G. will have them first thing in the morning."

"Once again, Jessica to the rescue!" Patrick said, and turned on the music. Immediately everyone jumped up and started moving to the sound.

Sean grabbed Olivia's hand and pulled her to her feet. "Come on, let's dance. Worktime is over."

Olivia allowed herself to be swept up, and tried to get back in the party spirit. She had been delighted that everyone had reacted so favorably to her article, but at the last minute Jessica, once again, had been the heroine. Why should I care, she wondered, since Walt's not here to witness Jessica's new triumph. She held tightly to Sean, who danced her around with the same smoothness and ease that he kissed. If she tried hard enough, she thought, maybe Sean would help her stop worrying about Walt and Jessica.

CHAPTER

The week dragged while everyone waited for the cheerleader mixer. But finally, it was Saturday evening.

Nancy's parties were famous for being the best in town. There was always plenty of food, plus the hottest new records and a great stereo system to play them on.

The only person on the guest list who was not looking forward to the big bash was Olivia. She and Nancy had had their differences all year long. They had been rivals for acceptance on the squad. And once, before Olivia started going with Walt, they'd even been rivals for the same guys.

That was all in the past, but Olivia still couldn't quite get over feeling nervous about being on Nancy's turf. Everything about Nancy Goldstein was just a little bit too perfect. Her clothes. Her parents' decorator-furnished house. Even her bouncy, fifty-dollar haircut.

Maybe, thought Olivia, I'm just jealous of Nancy because of her parents. Mr. and Mrs. Goldstein thought everything their little girl did was just great. They couldn't have been more supportive. What a contrast to Mrs. Evans, who always seemed to be doing her best to hold Olivia back.

Then, too, there was another reason why Olivia was sure Nancy's party was going to be a disaster. Jessica! The thought of spending an evening with Walt in the presence of that girl made her want to scream!

"Why don't we skip the party and spend the evening together at your house," Olivia suggested when Walt picked her up on Saturday evening.

Walt blinked in surprise. "Why would we want to do that? This is going to be a *great* party. Have you lost your mind?"

"But we could have a great evening alone, too," Olivia said. "Just the two of us."

"Sure," agreed Walt. "But we can do that any old time. This party is a one-time thing."

"Not really. Soon you'll be graduating and going away. How many evenings together will we have before that happens?"

"Olivia, why are we arguing about this? For one thing, we have to show up at Nancy's. It's a *cheerleader* mixer. What would it look like if two members of the squad don't even make an appearance?"

"The squad! That's your answer to everything!" Olivia shot back.

Walt started the engine of the Jeep, and sat there with his hand on the gearshift, looking glum.

"Olivia," he said. "Read my lips. I–am–going–to–this–party. You can come with me or not. Make your choice."

"Okay, okay. I'm coming," she agreed.

But it was not a very promising beginning to the big evening.

By the time they arrived at Nancy's house, the party was in full swing.

Walt was always in his element in large groups. He immediately started to circulate, telling jokes and exchanging a few words with everyone in the room.

Olivia, who lacked Walt's knack for small talk, made a beeline for Angie and Chris. She plopped down on the couch beside them and hoped, desperately, that they wouldn't desert her for the dance floor.

After twenty minutes or so, Walt had finished saying hello to everyone and made his way back to Olivia. "Come on, Livvy," he urged. "Let's dance."

"I don't think so," she excused herself.

She had already spotted Jessica in the room, looking fantastic in a white cotton dress that showed off her slender waist and pretty shoulders. Jessica looked so great and moved so well that Olivia dreaded having to be on the same dance floor with her.

"Why don't we go into the den," she suggested to Walt. "They're playing Trivial Pursuit in there."

Walt was beginning to think that Olivia was trying to spoil the party for him. "If you want to sit around playing some board game, fine," he said. "I'm here to dance. And if you won't dance with me, I'll ask someone else."

Olivia watched in misery as Walt headed for Jessica and led her out into the center of the floor. Deep down inside, she knew that the way she was acting was responsible for driving Walt straight into Jessica's arms. But she was angry with him, too. If he really loved her, wouldn't he have cared more for her feelings than for this dumb party?

Nancy had missed Walt and Olivia's little tiff because she was out in the kitchen, taking care of the food.

She had just put a tray of bite-sized pizza snacks into the oven and was waiting for them to get warm when Sean showed up.

"Even if you are the hostess, you're much too fun to be hiding out here in the kitchen," he said.

"Thanks," answered Nancy. "But try to tell that to the hungry crowd in the other room. They're eating everything in sight. If I don't get some more food out there soon, they'll probably start munching on the drapes."

"Who cares about them?"

Sean rested his hand on the small of Nancy's back. "Why don't we leave the crowd behind and run away together? Just the two of us."

"A flattering offer, but not very practical. Sorry."

"Why not?" persisted Sean. "You know, I've always been extremely attracted to older women."

Nancy laughed in spite of herself. "That's the first time I've heard that line."

123

"It's pretty clever, if I do say so myself," Sean said unabashedly. "But I'm serious. How about it?"

Nancy moved out of Sean's reach. "Not a chance. You may not have noticed, but I'm with Eric tonight. You remember Eric, my *boyfriend*."

"I've noticed. And honestly, Nancy, if you weren't a senior, I'd never try to come between you two. The thing is, I've had this wild crush on you all year long. And now that I realize you're graduating, I may never have another chance to tell you how I feel about you. Normally, I'd never put a move on another guy's girl friend.

"But y'know," he added, moving close again, "I think I'm in love."

Nancy laughed, but down deep she was flattered. It wasn't every day that you heard a declaration of love like that, and Sean was an adorable-looking guy.

"I do like you," she told him. "But I'm afraid fate is against us. And Eric and I are definitely a couple. At least for now. Sorry."

Sean departed with a wounded look in his big brown eyes, and Nancy returned her attention to the job at hand. Smiling to herself at Sean's unexpected confession, she removed the tray of hot snacks from the oven and transferred them to a serving dish, working fast to keep from burning her fingers.

Nancy delivered the plate of food to the main room, then returned to the kitchen and fixed a second dish for the group in the den. No doubt that was where she'd find Eric, who could never resist a chance to organize a marathon Trivial Pursuit tournament.

Nancy started down the hall towards the den, then stopped short in amazement. There was a couple standing in the recess behind the stairs, deep in conversation. The girl was Olivia Evans, but the guy was far too tall to be Walt.

She hated to give in to the temptation to eavesdrop. But then, if you couldn't eavesdrop in your own house, where could you?

Still frozen with indecision, she suddenly realized that the guy's voice belonged to Sean Dubrow. She couldn't stop herself from listening in.

"Normally I'd never try to come between a girl and her steady boyfriend," Sean was saying. "The thing is, I've had this wild crush on you all year long, Olivia. I think I'm in love."

"Me? Are you sure?"

Olivia sounded so stunned that Nancy almost gave away her presence by laughing out loud.

"Of course I'm sure," Sean persisted. "Don't you feel just a little bit the same way?"

Tell him no, Livvy, Nancy urged silently. Tell him to get lost.

"I do like you," Olivia said slowly.

Then she added, "Honestly, though, I hardly even know you. Besides, I'm with Walt tonight, and he's driving me home."

Olivia didn't sound completely sure about that last part. For all she knew, she'd already messed things up so badly with Walt that he didn't even

125

want to drive her home. But she wasn't going to add to the mistakes she'd already made this evening.

Olivia turned to go, and Nancy ducked out of sight around the corner of the staircase. Then, before Sean could slip away, she hurried to confront him.

"I'm tempted to dump this whole plate of food right on your head," she hissed at him. "The only reason I'm not going to is because you aren't worth wasting good food on."

Sean looked completely bewildered. "Nancy! What's the matter? Why would you do that?"

"What do you mean, *why*? I believed you when you said you had a crush on me. I felt good about it. But you didn't mean what you said at all."

"But I did!"

"No you didn't!" Nancy shot back. "And furthermore, you didn't wait five whole minutes before trying out the very same line on the next girl who came your way. You can't have a crush on every girl in school, Sean Dubrow."

Nancy sailed off in the direction of the den without waiting for a reply. Suddenly, she wanted very much to be with Eric, even if it meant missing out on the dancing in the living room to watch a bunch of people play Trivial Pursuit.

Sean watched Nancy go, hoping he hadn't made an enemy forever. The thing was, he *did* have a crush on every girl in school. Well, almost every girl. He knew it wasn't supposed to be that way, that a lot of girls thought he was being insincere and pushy. But when he got close to a gorgeous female, he just couldn't resist telling her how he felt.

My problem, thought Sean, is that no one appreciates a lover. All I want is to make girls happy, and they have to go and make everything so complicated.

The thought bothered Sean for at least a few minutes. Then he noticed Hope Chang standing quietly by herself near the door to the living room. She looked so serious and cute in her print skirt and white ruffle-sleeved blouse.

Sean ran his fingers through his thick curly hair, and arranged his face into a casual smile.

"Hey, Hope," he said. "Would you like to dance?"

CHAPTER

On the morning after Nancy's party, Jessica Bennett woke up early. She did a few quick limbering-up stretches, then hurried downstairs just in time to join her two brothers in the kitchen.

John was about to pour himself a bowl of dry cereal when Jessica showed up. "Wouldn't you rather have a cheese omelet and raisin toast?" she asked, taking the box out of his hand. "There's a loaf of home-baked raisin bread in the freezer. All it needs is a quick pass through the microwave."

"Sure," John agreed happily. "I can always go for a Jessica-special omelet."

"Count me in," said Gary. He had already had juice and a piece of toast an hour earlier, but he could always go for an encore when it came to meals.

Jessica found a big hunk of cheddar cheese in

the refrigerator and contentedly set to work grating it for the omelet. John fetched the paper from the porch, and he scanned the sports section while Gary cracked eggs into a bowl.

It wasn't often that the three of them had breakfast together. Gary, who was in the army, had been away from home most of the past year, stationed at a base on the West Coast. John went to the local community college and lived at home, but his schedule was so full that Jessica hardly ever got to spend time with him anymore. John usually went straight from classes to his part-time job, so he was seldom around for dinner. And when he wasn't working, he usually had to study late in the library, or else he was out on a date.

A few minutes later, Jessica was serving up three portions of perfectly done omelet while Gary helped her out by slathering butter on the thick slices of toast. "Isn't this great?" Jessica sighed, as she settled down at her place. "The three of us together. Just like old times."

"Better than old times, if you ask me," said John between bites of toast. "Remember when you decided you were going to learn how to cook, Jess? There was so much burnt cheese over everything that sometimes it was hard to tell the omelet from the pan it was cooked in."

"Right," agreed Gary. "In fact, the pan tasted better."

"And the loaves of bread you baked were hard enough to use as footballs," added John. "We used to toss them around in the backyard!"

"Stop it, you two," protested Jessica. "You guys are so cruel!"

129

But of course, she didn't mean it. Jessica secretly loved it when her older brothers teased her. And when she felt in the mood, she could more than hold her own in dishing out teasing in return.

The three Bennetts were much closer than most brothers and sisters. They had to be, because they'd been forced to depend on each other to get along. It was seven years now since their dad had died quite suddenly of a heart attack. Their mother, Abby, had taken the shock hard.

Abby Bennett had never really been able to talk about her grief over her husband's death. She did her best to be a good mother, and she'd worked hard at her job selling dresses at Marnie's to support the family. But for a while she was so emotionally distant that sometimes it almost seemed to Jessica that she'd lost her mother as well as her father. Thankfully, though, Abby had finally begun to open up, and Jessica felt close to her again.

Then, during Jessica's sophomore year, her mother had remarried. Jessica knew she should feel pleased about this. Her mother must have been terribly lonely, and she had no right to expect Mom not to find another husband. Still, she'd never quite gotten over resenting her stepfather Daniel for taking Dad's place. Sometimes, when Gary and John weren't around, Jessica almost felt as if she were an uninvited guest, a stranger in her own house intruding on Mom and Daniel's privacy.

This morning, she'd almost managed to forget for a few minutes that Daniel existed at all. After she and her brothers were finished eating, Jessica scraped and stacked the dirty dishes. Then she put on a pot of coffee, knowing her mother liked to have a cup or two to drink while she read the morning paper.

Well, no illusion could last forever. Just as Jessica finished measuring out the coffee, her stepfather entered the room. As usual, he was carrying a stack of computer printouts under his arm. Daniel worked for a company called Computer Systems, and it seemed to Jessica that he considered *any* time spent away from a computer terminal a *waste* of time.

"If that's for Abby, don't bother," he said. "She's left for work already. It's end-of-season inventory day."

"Oh, okay." Without further greeting to Daniel, Jessica pulled the plug on the coffee maker.

"How was the party last night?"

"Okay," mumbled Jessica again.

"I bet you knocked 'em dead in that dress."

"Huh?"

"I *said*," Daniel repeated, "I bet you knocked all the guys' eyes out in that new dress of yours. It cost plenty, but you looked very pretty."

"Oh."

"Did I say something wrong again?" Daniel asked. "Maybe the party didn't go so well."

"No, it went all right."

"So what's wrong?"

"Nothing at all." Why must you *always* bring money up, she thought.

Daniel frowned and buried his head in his papers. He kept trying to get through to Jessica, but it was like trying to make friendly conversation with an iceberg.

Jessica, for her part, was sure that Daniel only wanted her to find a boyfriend so she'd be pre-occupied — and out of his hair. If that happened she wouldn't be around much, and Daniel would have her mom almost all to himself.

The truth was, she was in no hurry to fall in love with anyone. Her Mom had loved her father, and that had only led to her being terribly hurt when Dad died. Mom probably loved Daniel, too, though Jessica couldn't see why. And *that* had led to her bringing him into the family, an outsider who kept trying to play father when he had no right to.

Getting involved romantically was just the first step to getting hurt, Jessica figured. Love couldn't keep a guy from leaving you. It hadn't kept her father from dying, either.

Still, on a strictly friendly basis, she got along well with the guys at school. Since she started trying out for cheerleading, Pres, and especially Walt, had been very nice. Very helpful.

The girls on the squad were a different story. Ever since the fashion show, they all hated her, and it wasn't her fault at all. Her mother and Mrs. Gunderson had corralled her into taking part as a model. She hadn't known that the other girls considered the show a Varsity Squad project.

Based on ability alone, Jessica knew her chances of making next year's squad were as good as anyone's. But the judges looked for more than just athletic ability. Surely, Coach Engborg and the others would see that the other girls didn't like Jessica — that they'd pegged her as a trouble-maker.

Daniel, still seated at the breakfast table with his morning cup of tea and his papers, almost seemed to read Jessica's mind. "By the way," he said mildly, "how are the cheerleading tryouts going? I bet you're good enough to teach some of the regulars a trick or two."

Irrationally, Jessica felt as if Daniel must be trying to goad her. "What do you know about it?" she snapped at him. "You don't understand anything at all!"

"*What* did I say now?" Daniel muttered.

Jessica didn't answer. She rushed out of the room, in a hurry to get away before Daniel could see how upset she was.

Rob Reynolds, on the other hand, had enjoyed Nancy's cheerleader mixer far more than he would ever have dreamed possible.

Rob had never thought much of his chances for snaring one of the two slots for guys on next year's Varsity Squad. He was basically a loner, a rough and ready, outdoor type with Walt Manners' compact build, but without Walt's outgoing personality.

Rob had always longed to play sports, but somehow he'd never found his niche in the Tarenton High athletics program. At five-six and 150 pounds, he was too small and not quite aggressive enough for football. Too short for basketball. Too short-legged and stocky to be speedy enough for track. And when the weather was good, Rob helped his dad in the family carpentry business, a commitment that kept him busy on Saturdays and ruled out playing baseball.

On his own, Rob loved hiking and climbing and canoeing. He and his dad went camping in Canada every summer and had a great time together. At school, though, he was mostly at loose ends. He wasn't even sure he wanted to be a cheerleader. He'd started hanging around at the tryouts mostly for something to do.

When the invitation to Nancy's party arrived, Rob hadn't expected much from that, either. He didn't care much for parties and didn't know how to talk to girls. Still, he'd been flattered enough to be included, so he'd shown up at the Goldstein house out of politeness.

For most of the evening he stood around in a corner of the living room, sipping a Coke and watching the others dance. These were the popular kids in school. Seniors like Pres Tilford and Mary Ellen Kirkwood. And Angie Poletti and her boyfriend Chris. And juniors like Sean Dubrow, who was dancing with the smartest girl in the class, Hope Chang. Rob felt a little bit out of his league.

He thought he was doing a pretty good job of being inconspicuous. So he was stunned when Holly Hudson, of all people, came up and asked him to dance.

Holly was dressed in clothes that announced her determination to be the sophisticated, artistic type. She was wearing a simple black dress that was little more than a knee-length T-shirt. But she'd topped off the effect with gobs of costume jewelry, two sets of earrings in her double-pierced ears, and more eye makeup than Queen Nefertiti ever wore.

"Come *onnn*! Don't tell me you're scared of me," Holly had urged.

So, reluctantly, he led her onto the floor and did a few awkward steps to a fast number, feeling that the whole room must be staring at him. As soon as the song ended, he mumbled something about not being much of a dancer and retreated to the sidelines.

"I wouldn't blame you if you were scared," a girl's voice coming from behind him said. "Parties always scare me."

"Me, too!" he blurted out in relief.

Rob looked around and discovered that he was talking to Samantha Gray. Cool, blonde Samantha. A girl he had daydreamed about, but never expected to actually have noticed him.

"How could *you* be scared of a simple party?" he exclaimed. "I mean, you're so popular, half the guys I know are afraid to talk to you!"

"Right," said Samantha.

They both laughed.

"I guess I get the picture," said Rob.

He was tempted to just shut up and retreat into his shell. But for once, he decided, he was going to take a chance. "Do you like walking?" he asked. "Maybe you and I could go for a walk tomorrow? How about it?"

When Samantha agreed Rob was so excited about his good luck that he could hardly sleep all night long. He was so glad he'd gone to the party.

But the next morning, when he picked up

Samantha at her house, he felt right away that the date was not going to be a total success. Samantha came out of her house dressed in white cotton slacks and a baby-blue cotton sweater that looked as if it would snag if you so much as came close to it. She was wearing matching baby-blue running shoes, okay for hiking, except that they were so new they hadn't even been broken in yet.

Rob guessed that Samantha was not exactly the outdoor type. Still, he'd invited her for a hike, and he couldn't think fast enough to come up with a new plan. Besides, Samantha would probably be insulted, or think he was just plain dumb, if he suggested a change.

They drove to the hills just outside of town, and Rob parked next to the foot of the Tupper's Hill path. Rob considered the path an easy one — it promised a short, but brisk, climb and a romantic, panoramic view at the top.

At first, things went well enough. Samantha groaned in dismay the first time she stepped into a muddy part of the path, dirtying her clean shoes. But she was in good condition, and she had no trouble at all keeping up with the pace Rob set.

Near the top, the dirt path came to an end. To reach the summit of the hill it was necessary to climb up over a series of rocky outcroppings. Rob had forgotten about this part of the hike when he chose this particular path. He loved climbing around on rocks, but he could see from the expression on Samantha's face that she didn't share his enthusiasm.

"You're kidding!" she gasped when she saw

what was ahead. "I'll get my clothes filthy. Besides, I'm terrified of heights. You said *walk*, not climb."

"I'm sorry I misled you. We can turn back here if you want," offered Rob, polite but regretful.

"No, it's okay. Lead on."

Samantha was determined to be a good sport. Rob was having a great time, scampering across the rocks like a mountain goat. She followed behind, gingerly moving from one safe foothold to the next.

At last they reached the top. Rob sat down on the huge, flat boulder that formed the summit of the hill, motioning for Samantha to sit beside him.

"Isn't this fantastic?" he enthused.

"Sure is," she agreed with relief.

They sat together for ten minutes or so, resting and taking in the view. Samantha looked achingly pretty, her cheeks flushed pink from the exercise. Rob wanted to put his arm around her and kiss her, but he didn't have the nerve. In fact, he couldn't think of a thing to say.

Finally he stood up awkwardly. "Guess it's time to go," he announced.

"Uh, just one question. How do we get down?"

"Same way we came up. Naturally."

"That's what I was afraid you'd say."

Samantha had been able to control her fear of heights on the way up. At least then she'd been *facing* the mountain, so she could forget about what was below her. Now, looking down, she was terrified. She knew it was crazy, but her whole body was shaking.

This isn't fair, she thought. When Rob invited her for a walk, she'd pictured a nice stroll in the park. Not this!

Trembling, she made her way down the way they had come up. She wasn't very graceful, but she managed to get as far as the last big boulder which jutted out about five feet above the dirt path.

"Now what?" she asked Rob.

"Jump," he said, demonstrating the move by leaping sure-footedly down onto the path.

Beyond the path there was a steep slope covered with a thick layer of wet leaves. Samantha pictured herself overshooting the path and sliding right down that slope, out of control.

"Come on," urged Rob. "It's easy. I've seen you make harder jumps than this in practice. Plenty of times."

"That was different."

"Why?"

"For one thing, my knees weren't shaking. Besides, I'm sure to land on my backside and ruin my slacks."

"Tell you what." Rob held out both arms. "Pretend you're coming down from a shoulder stand. I'll catch you. We did it just the other day."

Samantha really had no choice. She closed her eyes tight and jumped.

She landed neatly enough in Rob's outstretched arms. But in her panic she grabbed the back of his shirt, pulling it into a chokehold. Rob gasped and staggered a little.

Samantha responded by flailing her legs wildly

and clutching at Rob's throat with her other hand.

"Ughh . . ." he protested futilely as he toppled over backward.

Samantha rolled free and landed in a mound of wet, slimy leaves. She scrambled to her feet, unhurt but covered with grime. A small twig had caught onto the arm of her sweater, pulling loose almost a whole row of stitches and leaving a small tear in the elbow. Worst of all, she felt mortified. She was used to being cool, pretty Samantha. Instead, she was embarrassed and humiliated.

"Look what you did!" she accused out of anger, showing the torn sweater to Rob, who was sitting on the ground looking stunned. "Look at me! You've ruined my outfit! You practically got me killed!"

"I'm sorry, Samantha. Really I am."

"Well, okay. Forget it. But do me a favor and stay out of my way from now on."

Rob could hardly believe what a mess he'd made of things. Only yesterday, Samantha Gray had barely known he existed. Now, less than two hours into their first date, she couldn't stand the sight of him.

The worst of it was he had twisted his ankle when he fell. He limped down the hill and drove Samantha back to her house in silence, hoping she wouldn't notice the way he winced in pain every time he had to push in the clutch. Not only had he lost the girl, but he was pretty sure he'd blown his chances of making the squad as well.

CHAPTER

As Monday's practice got under way, it became obvious that the tryout picture had changed somewhat. Eight new candidates had shown up, attracted by the success of Nancy's party.

Rob Reynolds, for the time being at least, had dropped out due to a sprained ankle. He appeared at the gym to make his excuse to Coach Engborg and stared glumly at the early comers who were practicing stretches on the mats. Then he hobbled away.

Also among the missing was Olivia Evans.

Olivia hadn't dared to let the coach know that she wasn't going to show up, and Ardith Engborg was deeply annoyed.

"Does anyone happen to know where Olivia is?" the coach asked the seniors. "Or doesn't she feel the need to reveal her plans to anyone?"

Everyone shrugged and looked blank, even

Walt Manners. Over the weekend, he and Olivia had talked over her doubts about going out for cheerleading next year. But he couldn't see any point in sharing this news with the coach. Mrs. Engborg was more upset than he'd seen her in a long time, and he would only make things worse by opening his mouth.

"What's up with Livvy?" Mary Ellen whispered to Angie as soon as the coach turned her back.

"Who knows?" Angie looked blank.

"I don't understand that girl," Mary Ellen said. "She could be captain of the squad next year. The job is here for the taking. All she has to do is not goof up. Instead, the way things are going, she'll be lucky if she makes the squad at all. She's doing a pretty good job of convincing Ardith that she's completely irresponsible."

"Don't be too hard on her, Mary Ellen," said Angie. "Maybe Olivia has other things on her mind."

"Like what?" Mary Ellen brightened, hoping to hear that Olivia's problems were only temporary.

"Search me," Angie said disappointingly. "I've never really understood Olivia.

"One thing I do *know*," added Angie. "Holly isn't going to waste any time stepping into the gap left by Olivia's absence."

Sure enough, Holly was already talking to Coach Engborg, volunteering to help by working with the newcomers.

"I can practice my tryout routine on my own time," Holly said. "And I *do* know the basic cheers cold."

141

"Since the entire squad isn't present," the coach said pointedly, "I accept the offer."

"Some nerve," Angie said under her breath.

Holly heard the comment and decided to ignore it. With her dance background, she had more performing experience than anyone here, including the members of the Varsity Squad. It was just natural that she should emerge as a leader.

Secretly, she was sure that she would not only make the squad but get elected captain. She certainly deserved the honor more than that little mouse, Olivia Evans, even if Olivia *had* been on the squad for a whole year already.

Holly organized the newcomers in two lines and led them in a locomotive, the cheer that Mary Ellen invariably led at the end of every pre-game warmup. One thing you had to give Holly credit for: Her voice carried. All other activity in the gym came to a halt as Holly called out the letters of the cheer in a loud, penetrating yell. And at the end of the final line — "Go, Wolves, Go!" — Holly leaped high into the air, her back arched dramatically, and then fell into an effortless and graceful split.

A few of the newcomers applauded timidly, and Sean Dubrow joined in the response with a piercing whistle of appreciation. Instinctively, Holly turned to bask in the applause, doing a little bow that was only half in fun.

Mary Ellen had had as much as she could take. "The point of all this is to get the crowd to cheer for the team, not for *you*, Holly," she said sarcastically.

"You're just jealous," Holly shot back instantly. "Don't take it out on me because your day in the limelight is over."

"That's quite enough," Coach Engborg interjected.

Mary Ellen waited confidently for the coach to defend her. Instead, Ardith Engborg said crisply, "I think each of you owes the other an apology."

None too enthusiastically, Mary Ellen and Holly exchanged "I'm sorry's."

Mary Ellen felt betrayed. As the bustle of practice resumed, she retreated to the side of the gym, where Nancy and Angie were spotting some of the juniors doing tumbling runs.

The coach saw Mary Ellen there, and made a beeline across the floor. "You may have been right about Holly showing off a little," she said quietly. "But surely you see that it wasn't appropriate to undermine her in front of the entire group. I thought you'd learned more about leadership this year than that."

Mary Ellen held her tongue, but she could feel her cheeks burning. "Can you imagine Holly accusing me of being jealous?" she hissed to Angie. "What a joke! Why would I be jealous of *her*?"

Angie arched one eyebrow in skepticism.

"Come on, seriously," Mary Ellen persisted. "Why?"

"Why not? I am," Angie confessed. "I mean, I'm happy to be graduating. Still, it's a little bit scary to see how easy it's going to be for all these kids to take our places."

Angie had already given this subject some thought. She had nothing to complain about, but she wasn't a stunning beauty like Mary Ellen. And she didn't have a fantastic figure like Nancy, either. No matter what she did in the future, she was pretty sure that she'd never get as much attention as she had leading cheers for Tarenton High.

Not that there's anything so terrible about that, Angie told herself. There was more to life than being the center of attention at games. Still, there were moments when the realization did hurt a little bit.

"It's different for you, of course," she hurried to assure Mary Ellen. "You have a career ahead of you. Modeling and doing all kinds of exciting things. I wish I had your self-confidence."

"Thanks," Mary Ellen said hastily. "But I'm not all that confident."

Mary Ellen was sorry she'd ever gotten involved in this particular conversation. Lately, she'd been trying to avoid thinking about her plans for the future. She was every bit as scared as Angie. Maybe more.

The only difference was, she wasn't going to let herself brood about her fears. She was planning to enjoy every last minute of her senior year. When it was over, there would be plenty of time to make all those big decisions she'd been putting off.

After forty minutes or so, Ardith took over leading the practice, instructing the junior guys on the fine points of managing lifts, while the girls took turns partnering them.

Walt and Pres, who weren't needed for the time being, retreated to seats in the bleachers where they got into a conversation about the merits of the cheerleader hopefuls.

"It'll be too bad if Rob's ankle doesn't heal," observed Walt. "Without him in the running, Sean and Peter don't have much competition."

"That's true," agreed Pres. "The question there is whether Sean can manage to stay out of girl trouble until tryouts are over. If he can't, the coach could have a tough time putting together a coed squad."

"Look who's talking about girl trouble!"

"Exactly," agreed Pres pleasantly. "I speak from experience."

"Okay, then. Which girls do you think will make Varsity?"

Pres considered the subject. "Holly Hudson," he said. "Not that I like her that much. Her voice is awfully shrill, but she certainly seems to have captured the inside track. And then, I suppose, Sally and Betsey. They're both pretty good."

"What about Jessica?" asked Walt, a bit too quickly. "Seems to me she has it all."

Walt wished that he didn't have to feel guilty every time he just *thought* about Jessica. But he *did* feel that way, at least a little bit.

"I agree," said Pres, oblivious to Walt's feelings. "I think Jessica is very sweet, too. But for some reason, the other girls don't much like her. I'm sure Ardith must be wondering whether Jessica would be a disruptive influence."

Walt had this crazy urge to defend Jessica to

145

Pres, which made no sense at all. After all, it wasn't Pres who was against her.

"What about Hope Chang?" he asked instead.

"Perfect," said Pres. "Almost too perfect. Except for her soft voice. I can hardly hear her even when the gym is empty. Can you imagine what would happen in front of a noisy crowd? Hope is just too quiet to have the makings of a cheerleader."

"Probably," agreed Walt. "And then there's Tara Armstrong. What about her?"

Pres rolled his eyes in delight. "Something else," he said, conveying in his tone of voice that he had private knowledge of just how much else. Which, as it happened, he didn't at all.

Walt was vaguely aware that Pres was just putting on a front. But he was sensitive enough about his own lack of dating experience that he didn't have the nerve to call Pres's bluff.

"Right you are! And how!" Walt chimed in, doing his best to sound equally well-informed. "She could probably make it on her looks alone," he added.

"I'm with you there."

Tara just happened to hear the boys' conversation on the way back from the water fountain, and what she caught of this exchange made her seethe with anger. She wasn't a genius in the classroom like Hope Chang or a superb gymnast like Jessica. But it burned her up that so many people assumed that red hair and a great build were all she had going for her.

Sometimes, Tara even felt that if she had a

choice she would gladly change places with girls like Hope and Jessica. They didn't get as much attention as she did at first glance, but in the long run everyone seemed to sympathize with them, to go out of their way to make things easier. No one ever said "Poor little Tara."

Furthermore, guys like Pres and Walt acted as if they had some special claim to her, just because of the way she looked. They wouldn't snicker like that about any of the other girls.

It isn't fair, Tara thought. I have to fight for everything I want. But if that's the way it is, I intend to fight!

Returning to the gym floor, Tara took her place beside Hope, who was executing the steps of a fight cheer in quick, precise movements as Ardith called them out to the group.

"I just overheard Pres and Walt complaining about Holly's raucous voice," Tara said in a confidential tone. "That's one mistake I'll avoid when tryouts come around."

"Thanks for the tip," Hope said gratefully.

Hope had been worried about projecting her own voice, afraid that it was too soft and unauthoritative. Now she decided that she'd better be careful and not force it too much. She didn't want to sound shrill, after all.

The one candidate for next year's squad that Pres and Walt hadn't discussed was Olivia. Pres was as curious as anyone to know why Olivia had stayed away from practice, but he was too tactful to question Walt on the matter. Vanessa Barlow, on the other hand, was not burdened by an excess of tact.

Vanessa hadn't been at practice, of course. But her telephone grapevine was well organized. By that evening, when she happened to see Walt at the gas station in town, she'd already heard all about Olivia's absence from tryouts.

Catching sight of Walt as he was putting some air into one of his Jeep's front tires, Vanessa swung her mother's full-sized sedan next to the air pump and rolled down her window. "Hey there, Walt," she said, getting his attention. "Don't waste too much good air on those tires. Now that we're graduating, I'm sure you'll be wanting to move on up to a serious form of transportation."

"I doubt it," said Walt evenly.

"I guess you're right," Vanessa answered. "You *are* sort of the Jeep type."

"I'll take that as a compliment," offered Walt.

"Speaking of types, what's wrong with Olivia? I heard she's hiding out, avoiding the tryouts."

"She isn't hiding out," Walt said, not entirely sure that this wasn't true. "She just had to be somewhere else."

"No kidding? Where?"

"I don't know, Vanessa. What's the big deal?"

"Sorry," Vanessa commiserated. "I didn't mean to get into a touchy subject. It must be tough knowing that Olivia is keeping secrets from you."

Walt hung up the air hose and leaped up into the driver's seat of the Jeep. It was always a mistake to listen to Vanessa when she was pretending to be on your side. He wished he could just pull away and escape from this conversation, but Vanessa had blocked him in with her car.

Now, to make matters worse, she got out of the sedan and came over to the Jeep, leaning on the door in a way that made it look as if the two of them were having a very chummy conversation.

"I hate to mention it, but the Saturday before Nancy's party, Olivia was out with Sean Dubrow in his zippy black Mazda. I guess even Olivia likes fast cars — for a change of pace."

"If you hate to mention it so much, then don't. Do the world a favor, Vanessa, and have a zipper installed on that mouth of yours."

"You don't have to get nasty about it," Vanessa shot back, her cool facade deserting her.

She went back to her car and drove off in a huff.

Walt was so annoyed that he turned off the ignition by mistake, then almost flooded the engine getting it started again. Vanessa's troublemaking was so transparent that it was ridiculous to pay any attention to her. So why was it that she always managed to jab her needles in just the right spot?

Walt knew that there was nothing between Olivia and Sean now. She'd told him all about getting a ride from Sean that Saturday night, the night he was out of town for his grandmother's party. But what about next year?

Next September he would be away at school, while Sean would be right here, seeing Olivia every single day. Sean was an awfully smooth character. Could he really expect Olivia to ignore that?

It occurred to Walt that maybe he shouldn't try too hard to talk Olivia into staying on the squad. If she wasn't sure she wanted to be a cheerleader next year, then why argue her into it? At least, if she quit, she wouldn't be seeing quite so much of Sean Dubrow.

CHAPTER

At the Tilford mansion across town, the subject of a new car had also come up.

"I've been thinking," Mr. Tilford announced over the dinner table to Pres, "perhaps you would like a new car as a graduation present. Something a little more . . . substantial."

"There's nothing wrong with the car I have," Pres pointed out defensively.

That, of course, was an understatement. Pres owned the only red Porsche in Tarenton. He was the envy of the town, and the car was his pride and joy.

"I'm not suggesting you get rid of your sports car," Mr. Tilford assured him. "But it doesn't present quite the right image for a junior executive at Tarenton Fabricators. Also, you'll need a larger car to drive when you go East to Princeton. One with a trunk big enough to hold your luggage. I was thinking something along the lines of an Oldsmobile sedan. . . ."

"An Olds sedan," echoed Mrs. Tilford. "Very nice."

"Dad and Mom, I've tried to explain this before. Let's give it one more try. My plans are to stay here in town and work with Patrick Henley on building up our moving business. I'm not going to be working at Tarenton Fabricators this summer. And I'm definitely not going to Princeton, no matter how many strings you pull to get me admitted."

"But you *have* to go," Mr. Tilford thundered. "It's tradition!"

"That's right dear," Mrs. Tilford put in. "Tradition."

It infuriated Pres when his parents listened to everything he had to say, then dismissed it all as some sort of passing whim.

"There's another tradition you've told me about," he reminded them. "The one started by the first Preston Tilford. Remember how you used to tell me that he started the family business on one hundred dollars that he saved from raising chickens in his backyard? He started with next to nothing. Why is it so crazy of me to want to do the same thing in the moving business?"

Mr. Tilford was momentarily speechless. "Well," he said finally, "he *had* to do that. He had no choice."

"That's right," Pres's mom added helpfully. "He didn't have all this." She waved her braceleted hand around the room, drawing attention

152

to the antique silver, the oriental rugs, the mahogany furniture — and, last but not least, the view through the French windows of the Tilford's lakefront property.

"You must admit," she added with a small laugh, "it would be ludicrous to raise chickens here. They'd mar the landscape."

Mr. Tilford frowned. There were times when he suspected that his wife was only pretending to back him up while privately poking fun at him.

"Tell you what," said Pres, who was determined to escape before his parents forgot about him entirely and started arguing with each other. "If you insist on getting me a new vehicle for graduation, there's a secondhand truck for sale in Grove Lake that I'd really like to have. Patrick and I could use another truck, and it will be quite a bit cheaper than a new Olds. That's if you want to get me a present that *I* want. As opposed to what *you* want."

Pres left his dinner uneaten on the table, and went outside to his beloved Porsche. Lately, mealtime at home had become too tense to endure.

It was kind of funny when he thought about it, though. He lived in the biggest house in town, with gourmet meals prepared by a cook and served by a maid. Yet more often than not, he ended up having dinner at the Pizza Palace. Two slices with extra cheese, green peppers, and sausage.

Pres drove down to the Pizza Palace and was nearly finished eating his standard order when Jessica Bennett came in with two older guys.

Jessica noticed Pres as soon as she came in

and waved to him enthusiastically. "Hi, Pres," she hailed him. "Do you know my two brothers? Let me introduce you."

"Is that your Porsche out there in the lot?" Gary asked as soon as they'd been introduced. "It's really something."

The four of them trooped outside, and Pres opened the hood to show off the specially modified carburetor he'd installed himself. To his surprise, Jessica asked as many knowledgeable questions about the car as her brothers.

"Where'd you learn all this?" he asked her, amazed.

"From us, naturally," John said proudly.

"That's right," said Gary. "She's a great driver, too. I taught her myself."

"Maybe you'd like to drive this baby," Pres offered. "Tell you what, Jessica, I'll pick you up tomorrow, and you can take it for a little spin on the way to school."

Jessica's eyes glowed with happiness. "I'd love to," she gasped. "That would be terrific!"

When the Bennetts had gone back inside, Pres sat in his car, wondering what had come over him. He almost never let girls drive his car, especially around town. Maybe he was wrong, but he had this idea that once a girl started driving his car, she also began to think about going steady. Engagement rings and even wedding bells loomed somewhere down the road. And if she didn't think that way, everyone else in town did. The next thing he'd know, the word on the grapevine would be that Pres Tilford was seriously involved.

Pres's instincts told him that Jessica wasn't trying to snare him at all. She was cute and feminine, but she could also be one of the guys. She probably was more interested in his car than in him, much as his ego hated to let him admit it.

He just hoped that everyone else would understand that.

On Tuesday after school, Mary Ellen decided to put in a few hours working at Marnie's. She needed the extra money to pay for her prom dress, and Mrs. Gunderson had promised to let her work at the jewelry counter, where she'd earn a small commission on every sale.

Unfortunately, there were no customers to sell to. Now that warmer weather had finally arrived, everyone wanted to spend the late afternoons and early evenings outdoors. Marnie's was all but deserted.

Mary Ellen perched herself on a stool by the cash register, her attention focused on her English book which was discreetly out of sight on the shelf beneath the counter.

"I don't see anything here as pretty as you," a voice said very close to her ear.

Mary Ellen looked up and found herself nose-to-nose with Patrick Henley, who was leaning familiarly on the glass counter.

Patrick was, by his standards, quite dressed up. He was wearing freshly washed and pressed jeans and a light green workshirt that was neat, but obviously the veteran of many trips through the laundry. He smelled faintly lemony, an odor

Mary Ellen recognized as belonging to a good and very popular brand of men's cologne.

The sleeves of his shirt were rolled up to reveal muscular forearms that looked strikingly out of place resting above the delicate jewelry in the showcase.

"You can't hang around here," Mary Ellen said under her breath. "You'll get me in trouble."

"But I'm a customer," insisted Patrick.

"You are?" Mary Ellen looked doubtful.

"Sure. I'm looking for a present so special that it would convince this beautiful girl I know to stay right here in Tarenton, instead of running off to the big city in search of fame and fortune."

"Sorry. We don't have anything like that."

Patrick looked crestfallen. "That's what I was afraid of. Melon, I'd buy up everything in this showcase if I thought it would make you stay here in town with me. Including the rings."

"Patrick, please. You're only making this harder for both of us."

Mary Ellen couldn't tell Patrick what he wanted to hear, but she did agree to meet him outside when she finished work.

A few hours later, when she joined him in the parking lot, there was still an hour or so of daylight left. Patrick was driving the truck that he and Pres used for their moving company, the one with big letters on the side that read: H&T'S TLC MOVING.

Reluctantly, Mary Ellen hopped up into the passenger seat of the cab. She couldn't have felt more conspicuous if Patrick had asked her to ride

156

through town with him on the back of a circus elephant!

Mary Ellen had worked so hard to make Tarenton forget that she was a Kirkwood, one of the poor Kirkwoods who lived in the tacky little turquoise house on the wrong side of town. Not that she didn't love her family — she did! But she couldn't get over being embarrassed for their sake and hers.

So why had she ended up being attracted to the one guy in her class who seemed determined to embarrass her still further?

They rode in silence to the Overlook, a popular parking spot with a spectacular view of the length of Grove Lake.

"We can't stop here," Mary Ellen protested. "If anyone sees us parking in this humongous truck, we'll be the laughing stock of the town."

"What difference does it make?" Patrick asked. "Remember, in a few weeks you'll be off to New York. Why should you care about what people in Tarenton think?"

Mary Ellen couldn't think of an answer to that one.

"Confess," urged Patrick. "You haven't quite made up your mind about going, have you?"

"Yes I have."

Patrick leaned close and planted a long, passionate kiss on Mary Ellen's lips.

"Mind still made up?"

"Yes."

"Okay. Let's try again."

He started to kiss her a second time, but Mary Ellen pushed him away. "Why is it," she said,

157

"that every time you kiss me it's because you're trying to get me to promise to do something that I don't want to do? Because you want something from me."

Patrick threw up his hands in despair. "But I only want you. . . ."

"Only? This may be hard for you to grasp, but to me that seems like a lot."

"Forget it."

Patrick started the truck and backed it carefully out onto the main road. They drove in silence back toward town, with Mary Ellen staring pensively out the side window.

Patrick should have been thoroughly discouraged. But somehow, his brash self-confidence just wouldn't let him give up. "A penny for your thoughts," he said cheerfully.

"You don't want to know," Mary Ellen told him flatly.

"Yes I do," he persisted.

"Well, to tell the truth, I was thinking that I wish you were more like Pres."

"Ugh!" Patrick looked stricken. "Talk about a shot to the heart."

"You asked. . . ." she said guiltily.

"What you mean is," Patrick translated, "you wish I were rich."

"That's not it," she insisted, though to tell the truth she wasn't a hundred percent sure that Pres's money wasn't part of what she had in mind.

"Pres," she said after some thought, "has more perspective. He knows that there is life outside of Tarenton."

"That's what you think." Patrick grinned,

knowing that for once he had the power to tell Mary Ellen something that would shock her.

"What would you say," he went on, "if I told you that Pres is planning to stay right here in Tarenton after graduation? And not to work in the office at his father's factory, either. He and I are going to keep on with our moving business. So Pres Tilford will be getting his hands dirty, too, right along with me."

"You're kidding!"

"I am not. Ask him yourself."

Mary Ellen hardly knew what to make of this development. Am I crazy? she asked herself. Is there something wrong with me because I have all these ambitions? All these dreams?

There were times, especially when she was close to Patrick, that she felt sure the answer must be yes. So why was it that she could never quite put her dreams out of her mind?

CHAPTER

17

Unlike Mary Ellen, Angie didn't have the luxury of putting off making a decision about her future.

Angie had exactly two days left to send off a $250 deposit that would hold her place in the freshman class at State. Knowing how hard her mom worked to earn that much, she knew that she had better not change her mind once the money was in the mail.

The truth was, Angie was thinking that she'd just as soon not go to college at all. She had never been much of a student, and the thought of four more years in a classroom did not exactly fill her with joy. Besides, now that she had Chris, college seemed less important to her. She and Chris were right for each other. They'd probably marry in a few years and start having a family, and she didn't see how college would fit into those plans.

Anyway, Angie thought, she'd be happier at

home, helping out with the beauty shop that Rose Poletti operated from the basement level of her house. Her mother worked too hard, anyway, and Angie could take a beautician's course in Grove Lake that would qualify her in a few months.

To Angie's surprise, her mother was completely against this plan.

"I like Chris," Rose Poletti said when the subject came up. "But I won't have you planning your life around him. Even so-called perfect couples can wind up divorced today. And I hate to even mention it, but what if something happened and you ended up a widow like me?"

"I'm not planning my life around Chris," Angie argued back. "But even if I were, is that any worse than planning your whole life around some tragedy that may never happen?

"Besides," she added, "you didn't go to college, and you managed pretty well for us after Dad died."

Rose Poletti looked unconvinced.

"Furthermore," Angie put in for good measure, "college isn't necessary. A lot young people today are more interested in going straight into business. Look at Pres Tilford. He's thinking of skipping Princeton to go into the moving business. I talked to him about it just the other day."

Pres's example didn't make a dent in Mrs. Poletti's opinion. "You are not Pres Tilford," she said with finality. "You are my daughter."

Angie was still replaying that argument in her mind on Tuesday evening as she drifted around the supermarket, doing the family's weekly grocery shopping. She wasn't coming up with any brilliant solutions. So she felt relieved when she bumped into Carla Simpson in the canned foods aisle.

Carla was one of the underdogs whom Angie had taken a special interest in during tryouts. Actually, Carla was more than an underdog. Her routines were not that bad. Carla was athletic if not especially graceful. But with her chunky build, she just couldn't seem to move like a cheerleader.

But Carla's biggest problem was that she went through every practice looking as if she wanted to apologize to the world for existing. Sometimes Carla was so unsure of herself that she made the people around her uncomfortable.

Angie noticed right away that Carla's shopping cart was filled almost exclusively with low-calorie foods: diet soda, tomato juice, celery, and a few forlorn packages of frozen diet dinners. "Watching your weight?" she asked.

"Well, no," Carla lied, embarrassed. Then she grinned sheepishly. "Who am I trying to kid? I've been living on celery and carrots for days now. I'm determined to lose ten pounds by the day of tryouts, even if it kills me."

"Just be careful it doesn't," Angie warned. "You can take this crash dieting thing too far. Besides, I was just going to ask if you'd like to come over to my house. We could have a light dinner and go over a few cheers."

"Really?" Carla looked delighted. "That would be great. My mother is away for a few days, and it gets pretty lonely around the house."

"Isn't your dad home?"

"Oh sure," said Carla, "but he's not much company."

A few minutes later, they arrived back at the Poletti house. Carla stored her groceries in the refrigerator and Angie set out the makings of a dinner salad, in deference to Carla's diet. Then they went outside to the backyard and practiced a few cartwheels.

Carla may not have been graceful, but she was surprisingly strong. When Angie suggested that they do a few push-ups, Carla reeled off thirty-five without apparent effort. She might have gone on to do a few more, if Angie's brother, Andrew, hadn't shown up. "Way to go!" he said appreciatively, as Carla finished off the push-ups without so much as breathing hard.

"Andy, we're working on cheerleading stuff," Angie warned her brother. She didn't want him hanging around if it was going to make Carla uncomfortable.

"That's nice," said Andy, plopping into a lawn chair without taking the hint.

"Do you two know each other?" Angie asked, prepared to make introductions.

Carla nodded shyly, and Andy said, "Oh, sure. Carla's in my history class."

"You're the one who did that terrific project on ancient Greece," he added, speaking to Carla.

"Gee, thanks. You liked it, huh?" Carla's brown eyes sparkled with pride. Her whole face was transformed.

"Not only did I like it," said Andy, "but Mr. Graffman loved it. Which did not happen to be his feeling about my project. I have this problem with his course. I can't seem to figure out the difference between the Greeks and the Romans. They seem pretty much alike to me."

"You're kidding." Carla laughed.

"Would I kid about a thing like that?" Andy said. "Of course, if you were willing to take the time, you could probably help me to get the whole mess straight in my head."

"I'd love to," said Carla. She looked imploringly at Angie. "If you don't mind," she added.

"No, of course not," Angie said. "I'll fix us all something to eat and we can have dinner when you're finished."

"Great." Carla leaped up enthusiastically.

"To tell the truth," she said as she headed toward the house with Andy, "I could do these routines until my eyes pop out and I don't think it would help my chances of making the squad one bit."

Who knew that Carla was a history brain? Angie asked herself as she headed into the kitchen to work on the salad. Furthermore, she had a sneaking suspicion that Andrew was doing better in Mr. Graffman's course than he claimed. Was it possible that Andy was interested in Carla?

Some girls might have resented Carla for accepting an invitation to their home and then going off to spend time with their brother. Angie didn't mind, though. It made her feel good to see Carla looking so happy. And it was certainly a relief to see that Carla wasn't going to be completely devastated if she didn't make the squad.

It seemed to Angie that she was a lot better at working out other people's problems than her own. If only she were interested in something herself, the way Pres and Patrick were interested in their business, or Carla was interested in history. That would make planning her future a lot easier.

CHAPTER

Friday's practice rolled around, and this time Olivia showed up only to leave early. At least she had a good excuse for once: The staff of the school paper was holding an open meeting that afternoon to take nominations for next year's editors, and Olivia thought she just might attend.

Coach Engborg accepted Olivia's excuse without complaint, but it was clear from her expression that she was still unhappy with the lack of enthusiasm Olivia had been showing during practices for tryouts.

"I'm supposed to be impartial," Ardith Engborg said, "but I don't mind saying I'm disappointed in you. I know you've had a couple of problems this year, Olivia. But I thought you enjoyed being a cheerleader."

"Oh, I did," insisted Olivia.

"But you don't anymore?" the coach asked.

"I don't know. It's all going to be so different," Olivia stammered out.

And before they could discuss the subject further, Olivia bolted out of the gym.

After Olivia left, Walt spent most of the remaining hour working with Jessica on her routines. He tried to assure himself that his dedication had nothing to do with Jessica's green eyes or cute dimples. It was just that Jessica, who was such a good gymnast, would make a real difference on next year's squad.

As it happened, this was mostly true. Jessica was a first-rate tumbler, and completely fearless. She could pick up new tricks after just a few tries. She was, Walt thought more than once, a softer, more easy-going version of Olivia.

It's just my luck, thought Walt, that I prefer the original version. Olivia might be tiny, but that small body of hers was filled with stormy emotions. Sometimes he found it hard to cope with Olivia's continual crises. Still, he had to admit that anyone else, even Jessica, seemed like a pale copy of the real thing to him.

Walt was so busy thinking about Olivia, that he did a poor job of spotting Jessica on her last back flip in a series.

"Whoof," she exclaimed as she collapsed onto the mat, unhurt but startled.

"Sorry, Jessica."

"No problem," she answered as Walt helped her to her feet.

"You're a good sport." said Walt distractedly. "But I'm not in the mood for this stuff today. Why don't we take a break and have some juice from the machine out in the hall?"

Walt's exit with Jessica was noticed by the rest of the senior squad, who were quick to draw the obvious, but wrong, conclusion. After practice, as soon as the hopefuls had changed and cleared out of the locker room, Nancy joined Mary Ellen and Angie in speculating on just what was going on.

Mary Ellen, who still felt irrationally possessive about Pres at times, joined the trio in expressing their outrage at Jessica.

"It's just too much," Mary Ellen complained. "It's bad enough that she's throwing herself at Walt Manners. But do you know that she's after Pres, too? He's been picking her up in the mornings and letting her drive his car to school."

"That is nervy," Nancy agreed. "But the real problem, in my book, is that she's trying to break up one of the nicest couples I know."

Jessica, who'd been out in the hall listening to Walt all the while, entered the locker room just in time to catch Nancy's last statement. She wondered vaguely who Nancy and the others were discussing. Then, as she saw the trapped looks on all their faces, it dawned on her that she must be the person they'd been talking about.

"Do you mean *me*?" she sputtered.

"I didn't mean for you to overhear," Nancy admitted. "But since you did, I won't deny it. I think it's rotten of you to be chasing after Walt when you know that he's going with Olivia."

"And chasing Pres, too." Mary Ellen put in. "Surely you can't want them both."

Jessica was completely bewildered. *"Pres? Walt?"* she forced out. "But they aren't interested in me! We're just friends."

The other three girls looked disbelievingly at her.

Jessica felt herself starting to get angry. "You're all boy crazy, that's your problem," she blurted out. "I mean, what girl in her right mind would want to go steady and have some guy hanging all over her, getting jealous every time she made a move without his permission? If you ask me, it isn't worth it. All this love stuff is a trap ... leaving you open to being left."

After Jessica made her exit, Mary Ellen, Nancy, and Angie just sat there, staring at each other in amazement.

"If you ask *me*," Nancy said at last, "I think she meant it. Nobody could have delivered that speech with a straight face if it weren't the truth."

"Who would have thought?" Mary Ellen exclaimed. "Jessica Bennett doesn't like boys!"

"I don't think that's quite right," observed Angie. "She likes boys all right. Or she wouldn't be so defensive. It's just that she's scared of them. Or scared of commitment."

"If that's so," said Nancy, "then Olivia doesn't have anything to worry about. I know that that's been one of the problems on her mind lately. Won't she be relieved when she finds out that Jessica isn't interested in Walt, except as a friend! I can hardly wait to tell her!"

"Not so fast," Angie warned.

"Why not?" Mary Ellen wanted to know.

169

"Look at it this way," explained Angie. "None of this changes the fact that Jessica is really cute, and a good athlete, too. It's bad enough if someone like her is out to take your boyfriend and your place on the squad, too. But at least knowing that, you might feel like fighting back."

"So?" Mary Ellen and Nancy asked in unison.

"So," said Angie, "what we've figured out now is that Jessica isn't such a bad kid after all. At least she isn't purposely making a play for Walt, but that doesn't mean he won't be interested in her. And she also could win Olivia's slot on the squad."

Nancy groaned. "I see what you mean. If Jessica isn't causing trouble on purpose, that only makes the situation worse."

"I'm beginning to think that Olivia wasn't so lucky to make cheerleading in her junior year after all," said Angie. "She's spent all this year with us seniors. She hardly knows the kids in her own class. And if Jessica doesn't see Olivia as a target, she's probably the only girl in the group who doesn't. I promise you that when Holly and the others come to try out, every one of them is going to be mentally competing with Olivia. No wonder she's a little bit nervous."

Olivia was more than just a little bit nervous.

She and Walt were spending Friday evening at his house. Walt had planned the kind of quiet time together that Olivia had said she wanted the night they had to go to Nancy's party.

The two of them took a long walk in the cool pine woods that surrounded the Mannerses' architect-designed house, then snacked on cheese and crackers and grapes from the well-stocked kitchen before heading to the den.

Walt had borrowed some videocassettes of old Fred Astaire movies from one of the "techies" who worked at the TV station where his parents did their breakfast-hour talk show. He popped one of them into the VCR and sat back, entranced.

On the screen, Fred Astaire was doing a dance with a simple, straight-backed chair as a prop. At one point, he danced up onto the back of the chair and then rode it gracefully to the ground without missing a step, the chair back sinking under him so smoothly that it seemed to defy the laws of gravity.

"I love this stuff!" Walt crowed. "Isn't it great!"

Olivia wasn't quite so enchanted. The story was kind of silly, just an excuse to string together a bunch of dance numbers. And she just couldn't see Fred Astaire as a leading man. "He has weird-looking ears," she observed.

Walt didn't seem to think that was funny. "You *would* notice that," he groused. "The greatest dancer in history, and all you can see is that he isn't a hunk."

It occurred to Olivia that Walt was thinking about himself. Round-faced, short-legged Walt was another dancer who'd never look like a leading man no matter how good he became. "I'm sorry . . ." she began.

"Forget it," said Walt.

"Did I tell you," he added, "that the Red Hat

Theatre is going to be doing *Guys and Dolls* this summer? That's one musical that's sure to have a juicy part for me."

"What?"

"The Red Hat," he repeated. "I told you. I applied to apprentice there and I was accepted. The season starts July 4th weekend and lasts most of the summer."

Olivia did remember that several months ago Walt had talked about sending in an application for a summer internship at Red Hat, located in a summer resort on the shore of Lake Michigan. At the time, the summer had seemed remote. And she'd figured Walt probably wouldn't be accepted anyway.

"But that theater is a couple of hundred miles away!"

Walt had been dreading this discussion of his summer plans. He felt guilty, but also resentful that Olivia wasn't going to be happy about his success.

"I know, Livvy," he told her. "I'd love to spend the summer with you. But you can't expect me to sit around Tarenton all summer with nothing to do!"

"Who said you had to do nothing?"

"Be reasonable, Livvy." Walt squeezed her shoulder in a gesture that implored her not to be unhappy.

"It seems as if almost everyone I care about is leaving town. Even you," Olivia said. "They can't wait to get away. It's all they talk about. And I get tired of pretending to be thrilled for them when what I really feel is that I'm being kicked aside like an outgrown pair of shoes."

"Oh, come on. It's only for a year, and then you'll be thinking about leaving, too. And in the meantime, you'd lead the Tarenton Cheerleading Squad on to new heights of glory."

"I'm not even sure I want to do that," Olivia sniffed. "Those kids aren't my friends. And who's to say I'll even make next year's squad? Ardith is really down on me lately, and I haven't even worked up an individual routine."

"That's no excuse. You're good enough to breeze through tryouts, and you know it. We're counting on you to carry the torch for all of us."

Then Walt thought about Sean Dubrow. Sean would surely be on next year's squad — riding the bus with Olivia to all the away games . . . partnering her in lifts and routines . . . and, no doubt, driving her home from practice in his zippy black Mazda.

"Look," he said, "I'm not going to talk you into trying out if you don't want to. It's your decision, Livvy."

This wasn't what Olivia had been hoping to hear. Not only was Walt going away, he seemed to be serving notice that he didn't much care what she did once he was gone.

That night Olivia had a dream that was in black and white, like the old movie she and Walt had watched on the VCR.

Walt was doing a tap dance, dressed in a top hat and tails. At first, Olivia was his partner, whirling around as gracefully as Ginger Rogers ever had. Then the scene changed. Now Walt's partner was Jessica Bennett, dressed incongruously in the red skirt and white letter sweater of a Tarenton High Cheerleader. Olivia was stuck on the sidelines, watching the dance and thinking how silly it was of Walt to choose a partner who wasn't even wearing the right costume.

Then the scene changed again. This time, Olivia was in a huge train station — the kind she'd only seen in movies, never in real life. All the senior cheerleaders were going to catch a train, half running and half dancing, as if they were part of a movie musical production number. Everybody seemed wildly happy, especially Walt.

Finally, all of them were on board the train. Olivia could see herself standing alone on the platform, holding a big torch like the kind they used to open the Olympic games.

Olivia waved good-bye, but the passengers on the train had already forgotten about her. Or maybe the train's engine just drowned out their farewells. The engine was chugging away, and the noise it made was getting louder and louder by the second. . . .

Suddenly, Olivia opened her eyes and sat up in her bed. The nightmare was over, but the pounding was still with her. She realized, with a rush of fear, that what she was feeling was her own heartbeat.

Olivia felt panicky. This was exactly what her mother was always predicting: a return of the heart trouble that had kept her confined to hospital beds for so long when she was a child.

What if the nightmare hadn't been about graduation at all? What if it was telling her that she was going to die? Maybe that was why, in the dream, her friends hadn't seemed able to see her or hear anything she said to them!

Olivia went to the bathroom and got herself a glass of water. Then she returned to bed and concentrated on counting backward from one hundred. Eventually, her heart settled down, but she couldn't sleep for the rest of the night.

She kept thinking that she didn't dare let anyone know about her fears. If her mother found out about this incident, she'd never let her hear the end of it. Forget about cheerleading! Knowing Mom, she'd probably keep her practically under house arrest for senior year!

CHAPTER

Tara Armstrong was desperate.

She stood in front of the living room fireplace, hands on her hips, shaking her mane of red hair for emphasis. "This is a crisis!" she cried. "Can't you understand that? I can't show up for the tryouts in the same outfit I've been wearing to practice all along."

Her mother looked up from her magazine. "I don't see why not, dear," she said mildly. "That red leotard of yours is only a few months old. It's as good as new. You don't need a new one. Besides, it's only a tryout."

"*Only*! My whole fate is in the balance. Don't you see, either I'll be a cheerleader next year or I'll be just another nobody. Part of the faceless crowd. I've got to do everything possible if I'm going to win."

Mrs. Armstrong looked unimpressed. But Tara's father, who'd been listening to the argument from the comfort of his favorite chair, smiled at his daughter indulgently.

"Since it's so important to you, I think we can manage to afford to see you properly attired," he said. "Though if you ask me, what the young girls call exercise clothes these days would be more appropriate on the dancers in a nightclub chorus line."

Mr. Armstrong produced a wad of bills from his pocket, then his keys so that Tara could borrow the family car to drive to the shopping mall.

Tara immediately brightened. "Thanks, Dad," she said, giving her father a grateful peck on the cheek.

On the way out of the house, she passed through the kitchen where Marie, the housekeeper, was busy taking a batch of homemade brown-sugar cookies out of the oven.

"I think you worry too much," Marie said affectionately. "These judges will like you for yourself, Tara. They don't care so much about seeing you wearing a fancy leotard."

Tara sighed. "I appreciate the vote of confidence, Marie. But remember, you're prejudiced in my favor."

Giving Marie a hug, Tara grabbed a cookie and headed for the garage. Fortunately, one problem she didn't have to worry about was her figure. Still, she was worried about almost everything else. It didn't occur to her to take Marie's observations seriously. Deep down inside, Tara felt like an impostor. A nobody accidentally caught inside the body of a brassy redhead. Most of the time, the disguise seemed to work all too well.

Still, she was sure that someday, when she was most counting on her appearance to get her by, someone would notice the true Tara and call her bluff.

The Emperor's New Clothes! That was one story that Tara had no trouble relating to. She'd noticed that no one except her ever seemed to feel any sympathy for the emperor. You weren't supposed to, she guessed. He was just there to be made fun of.

On the drive to Pineland Mall, she reviewed the competition she was going to be up against. The picture had changed somewhat since the practices began, though Tara wasn't sure that the changes would help her chances all that much.

First, Olivia Evans, who had seemed like a sure thing in the beginning, seemed determined to self-destruct. The general opinion among the other candidates was that Olivia was scared of the competition, and was brooding over Walt's coming graduation. But Tara wasn't so sure. Though few people suspected it, Tara was a close observer of other people. And to her eyes, Olivia looked unnaturally pale, almost ill. At the very least, Olivia had something on her mind that she wasn't sharing with her friends.

Then there was Holly Hudson, who most of the girls still thought of as a leading contender. Tara had an idea, though, that Walt and Pres had been right about Holly. She was too bossy, too much of a show-off, and the judges would see that right away.

Even Jessica, the perfect cheerleader in looks

and talent, had problems. It was obvious that the senior girls didn't like her, and who could tell whether or not the judges would count this against her when it came to considering leadership and sportsmanship?

Even so, Tara felt sure that her own chances of making the final four group of girls were slim at best. Of the three girls she'd already considered — Holly, Jessica, and Olivia — at least one would probably slip into the winner's circle. Maybe two of them.

Then there was Samantha Gray. Tall, ash-blonde Samantha was so self-possessed that the judges probably wouldn't dare disagree with Samantha's own high opinion of herself. And sometimes it seemed to Tara that blondes had an inside track in everything. People assumed they were sweet, even if they weren't. Unlike redheads, thought Tara, who were considered "difficult" no matter what they did.

And Hope Chang. Hope was a born teacher's pet. The kind of girl adults always approved of — and whom Tara therefore automatically resented.

And Betsey and Sally. They were still threats even though their carbon-copy routines, courtesy of her own suggestion, weren't going to help their chances any.

Even Carla had started to look like a serious threat. Carla was much more relaxed than she'd been during the first days of practice, and ever since Rob Reynolds had gotten over his sore ankle, the two of them had been practicing lifts together a good deal. Coach Engborg had noticed both of them and had commented more than once that Carla was the most improved of all the candidates.

Tara had heard that besides Coach Engborg, two of the other four judges were going to be the assistant basketball coach, and Mrs. Strickland, the other girls' gym teacher. Mrs. Strickland taught girls' swimming and diving, and she was sure to see that Carla was a good athlete.

By the time she reached The Dressing Room, the boutique that sold the best exercise clothes in town, Tara had pretty much convinced herself that she could never win except by some fluke — or at least not without a bit of scheming on her part. She got another unpleasant surprise when she saw none other than Hope Chang in the store, methodically picking over the selection of leotards.

"I see we both had the same idea," commented Tara, assuming a sugary voice that covered up her true feelings about the situation.

Hope was examining a pink- and black-striped leotard that dramatically complemented her exotic eyes and coloring. The design also served to emphasize that Hope was one girl who could afford to wear broad stripes without fear. Her hips were practically nonexistent. Bulge was not a word in Hope's vocabulary.

Standing next to Hope, Tara felt like a hippopotamus. Her own curvy figure seemed almost obscene.

"Don't you think the colors are a bit extreme?" she lied sweetly. "I think the judges would prefer something like that navy blue one."

"Oh, I don't know," Hope said. "I've always thought that navy blue makes my skin look sallow."

This was true, but Tara assured Hope that it wasn't so at all.

"Sean tells me that I ought to wear brighter colors," Hope persisted.

"Oh, Sean!" said Tara automatically. "Who pays any attention to anything Sean says?"

Hope looked upset. "Don't you like Sean?" she asked worriedly.

"Of course I like him. *Everybody* does. I just meant that it doesn't pay to take the things he says too seriously. Sean has a line for every occasion."

"I don't think so," Hope insisted tenaciously. "He seems like a very nice boy to me."

"Well, if you say so. I'm sure you must know," Tara said.

Hope relaxed. She had never dated much, except for the kind of meaningless dates that developed when members of her group paired off for a dance or other couples event. She had always been too shy, and too preoccupied with schoolwork and her family, to pay much attention to boys. But Sean Dubrow had been going out of his way to make her feel special. And he was so very handsome and popular.

Ever since the evening of Nancy's party, Hope had been wishing that she had a special friend among the girls, someone to whom she could confide her feelings about Sean. Tara Armstrong had never been Hope's idea of a potential best friend. But maybe she'd misjudged her.

"Sean has been paying a lot of attention to me these last few weeks," Hope confessed shyly. "I think he likes me. I've even been thinking that maybe he's going to ask me out."

Tara's eyes widened. Hope was even more naive than she'd thought!

Tara's first impulse was to laugh. Her second was to say nothing. Knowing Sean, chances were fair that he'd do something between now and the tryouts to break Hope's heart. As a matter of fact, Tara thought, with a little encouragement from me, Sean would be sure to disappoint Hope.

Tara swallowed hard. For once, she was going to be honest. Hope needed some sisterly advice.

"If I were you," Tara told her, "I wouldn't count too much on Sean Dubrow as boyfriend material. Go out with him, sure. Have a good time. But don't set yourself up to get hurt when Sean starts chasing some other girl. Sean enjoys playing the field too much to stick with any one person for long."

The smile on Hope's face hardened into an expression of hostility. "Thanks for the advice," she said icily. "But I'll make up my own mind about Sean."

Without further ado, Hope picked up the pink and black leotard and marched toward the cash register.

Tara was stunned. Here, for once, she'd tried to be unselfish and helpful, and look at the thanks she'd gotten! In the future, she'd remember that sincerity did not pay off.

* * *

And as far as Hope Chang was concerned, Tara was right.

Hope was not smart for nothing. She'd always been a little bit suspicious of Tara. And that evenning, she methodically thought over Tara's behavior since the beginning of practice. Inevitably, Hope remembered that it was Tara who had advised her not to try too hard to project her voice, for fear of sounding shrill. Realizing that Tara had set her up for a fall made Hope so angry that she wanted to scream.

You can bet I won't have any trouble making myself heard when tryouts come around. Hope promised herself. All I'll have to do is get out there on the floor and think of Tara Armstrong. The very image of that girl's face will make me so worked up that they'll hear me yell all the way to Grove Lake.

In the meantime, a few blocks away at Betsey's house, another of Tara's plots was unraveling.

Betsey, Sally, and Peter had gotten together that evening to go over the words to the basic cheers one last time. At Peter's suggestion, they also decided to critique each other's individual routines.

Even Sally, who'd been especially nervous about letting anyone see her perform, had agreed to go along. A little timidly, she went through the motions of the "Whomp 'Em, Wolves" cheer, then the Tarenton fight song. She dived into her tumbling routine, and ended with a back walk-over and a split.

"Oh no!" groaned Betsey loudly as Sally arched

her back and threw up her hands to signal the end of her performance.

Sally looked stricken. "Was I that bad?"

"Of course not," Betsey assured her. "It's just that I was planning to do the very same move. I didn't copy it from you, honest. But the judges would never believe that, I bet. Everyone knows we're friends."

Betsey was momentarily suspicious. Then she relaxed. "Come to think of it," she recalled, "it was Tara Armstrong who showed me that particular move. She said she wasn't planning to use it."

"That's right," Sally said. "Tara showed it to me, too.

"It must be an accident," Sally added. "I mean, I'm sure Tara wouldn't intentionally set us up to look dumb."

The two girls looked at each other, wondering.

"Let's not waste energy worrying about Tara," Peter said quickly. "Anyway, I have a lot of good ideas I haven't been able to use in my routine. I have enough material for both of you."

"Great!" said Betsey. "I'd rather start from scratch than polish something that will leave the judges wondering which routine is the original and which is the carbon copy."

CHAPTER

It was the day before tryouts, and Olivia was feeling more panicky than ever.

That evening at dinner, she sat in silence watching the gravy and mashed potatoes on her plate run together. The few bites she had already eaten had refused to settle into her stomach, sticking halfway down her throat in a hard lump. While her parents talked around her, Olivia tried to concentrate on deciding what she was going to do when tomorrow came.

For the last few days, Olivia had attended practice faithfully. However, she'd been too worried about starting her heart racing again to do much more than stand around watching the others work out. It seemed that she had spent a good deal of those sessions watching Walt and Pres coach Jessica. But for some reason, she didn't see that Mary Ellen, Nancy, and Angie were also upset about the situation.

Also, she'd noticed this funny ache in her chest that seemed to get worse the more she worried about it.

Strangely, except for that, and being tired from lack of sleep, she felt pretty good during the days. It was after she got home in the evenings that things got bad. Twice more, she'd awakened in the early morning hours to that awful feeling of her heart thumping like a runaway train.

Then today, it seemed that everything possible had gone wrong. She'd been so tired that she very nearly missed the bus and almost didn't make it to school at all. Then she picked an argument with Walt at lunchtime, all because he'd put mustard on her sandwich when she didn't want any. Then, during sixth period, Mrs. Knox had returned their algebra tests from the previous week, and Olivia's paper had come back marked with a big red "D" at the top.

"I just know you can do better than that, Olivia," Mrs. Knox said to her after class. "You seem so tense lately. Perhaps you'd like to take a makeup test in a few days, when you're more prepared."

Olivia found it hard to believe that Mrs. Knox would let anyone take a makeup exam. It was almost as if she were being treated as a special case. Maybe I haven't been doing such a great job of keeping a secret after all, Olivia thought. Maybe there is something seriously wrong and everyone knows about it but me — my parents, my teachers at school, everyone.

"You've got to eat, Olivia. To keep up your

strength," Mrs. Evans urged at that moment, as if to confirm her daughter's suspicions.

"Good grief, leave the girl alone," Mr. Evans snorted at his wife.

Olivia pushed her plate away. The idea that had started as a farfetched train of thought was starting to seem almost reasonable.

"I had a snack after school," she lied. "I guess that's why I'm not hungry."

Mrs. Evans sighed. "Very well. I'll save what's on your plate in case you want to heat it up later."

Olivia watched as her mother slid the mess from her plate into a plastic container and carefully sealed it with aluminum foil. Eating her mother's cooking was another of those things that she was supposed to do out of duty. And like most duties, she couldn't evade it — only put it off a little bit longer.

"I think I'll go out for a walk," she said.

"A walk?" Mrs. Evans's tone of voice would have suited just as well if her daughter had announced that she was going to reach the South Pole before sundown. She acted as if a simple walk sounded like a bizarre, even perilous undertaking.

"All right then, dear, but don't forget to wear your sweater," Mrs. Evans conceded.

Olivia was in no mood to argue. Obediently, she pulled on her sweater even though the weather was warm enough for short sleeves.

It was a relief to get out of the house, but then she had no idea where to go. Since the weather was so nice, a lot of people were sure to be out of doors and she was in no mood to run into any of her friends.

Over the last few days, Nancy, Mary Ellen, Angie, and even Pres had taken her aside and given her little pep talks on the subject of the tryouts. "I know you can do it," Angie had said. "You've got to uphold the honor of this year's Varsity," pleaded Mary Ellen. "You're a sure bet for captain," both Pres and Nancy had told her.

Even Walt had come up with that awful phrase about "carrying the torch." Oddly enough, however, he had been pretty noncommittal about the issue ever since. This was strange since Walt was usually the gung-ho type.

It occurred to Olivia that Walt's behavior might be one more piece of evidence that there was something wrong with her. If her parents had heard a bad report from her last physical, naturally they might let Walt in on the news, if only so that he could keep an eye on her.

Olivia decided to head for the old town park up on the hill. The little park was used by joggers occasionally, so it wasn't too deserted and no one would think it strange to see her there. On the other hand, in this weather, most kids would be over by the lake.

She walked briskly up the hill to the park, and was happy to find it momentarily empty. She had so much to figure out. For instance, if she did try out tomorrow, what was she going to do for a routine? In her mind, she worked out a few moves that might do. It certainly wasn't going to be as easy this year to impress the judges with her gymnastic ability. The competition on that score wasn't only from Jessica. It seemed that the example set by this year's squad had encouraged a lot of hopeful cheerleaders to work on their own skills.

Then there was the problem of Coach Engborg. Should she go to the coach and apologize for the way she'd been acting before the tryouts? No, it was too late for that. Ardith would just think that she was asking for special consideration that she didn't deserve.

The more Olivia tried to straighten things out in her head, the more upset she became. That funny ache had returned, and her face felt hot. She took her pulse and realized that it was racing — more than it should have been, even after climbing the hill.

It occurred to her that she'd been really dumb to come to a place where, if she became ill, no one would be around to help. She made her way back to the paved road, then headed down the steep hill as fast as she dared. Not until she passed the last bend in the twisting hill, and could see the town below her, did she stop briefly to rest.

Suddenly, she became aware of a noise coming from up the hill. A horn honked insistently, and she turned around just in time to see the H&T's TLC Moving truck barreling around the bend. She jumped out of the way and the truck came to a screeching halt just a few feet short of where she had been standing.

"Livvy, is that you? What do you think you're

doing, standing there in the road like that? Just past a curve, too! You could've caused an accident. It's a good thing I had the brakes fixed the other day."

Patrick Henley was so excited he couldn't stop yelling. Finally he calmed down enough to notice the look on Olivia's face. "Are you all right?" he asked.

"I guess so," she said. "It's just. . . ."

"Just what?"

"I don't know. My heart was beating so fast. It keeps doing that. For a minute I thought I was having some sort of attack. . . ."

Everyone knew that Olivia had suffered from heart trouble as a child. Just her mention of the word *heart* scared Patrick so badly that at first he didn't know what to do. "Don't move," he said. "Stay right there. Sit down. No, on second thought, we'd better get you to the hospital right away."

With that, he scooped Olivia up in his arms and lifted her into the cab of the truck.

Only minutes later — it seemed like seconds — they were careening into the driveway that led to the hospital's emergency entrance. Patrick ran inside and whatever he said to the person on duty there must have made a big impression. Two orderlies sprinted out the door, lifted Olivia onto a gurney, and pushed it inside at top speed. Olivia heard someone shout the words "Heart attack!" and someone else, sounding very upset, saying, "She's just a kid!" Then a nurse opened Olivia's sweater and blouse and blinked as she saw the

190

scar from her childhood operation. Someone else poked her chest with a stethoscope and pretty soon some sort of monitoring machine was being connected to Olivia's arm.

Everyone looked so worried that she was sure there was something dreadfully wrong.

After that, things calmed down a bit.

A woman in a white coat arrived and introduced herself as Dr. Graham. She looked worried, but less excited than the other staff as she explained to Olivia that there was going to be an EKG to test her heart, and then some X rays.

The tests were done, and Olivia was put into a small room off the main emergency room to await the results. The monitor was still attached to her, and every few minutes Dr. Graham stuck her head inside the door and gave Olivia an encouraging smile.

Olivia was starting to feel a good deal better, but she dreaded the results of the tests. She hated hospitals and felt sure that once you were inside one of them, the doctors would be sure to find things wrong with you. That was certainly the way it had worked when she was a kid.

Out in the hallway, she could hear the murmuring voices of her mom and dad, then Walt. She was sure she heard Dr. Graham's voice, too. The voices got louder when Walt and Olivia's parents demanded to be let in to see her.

"Not quite yet," said Dr. Graham. "Everything's under control, I promise you. But I want to complete our tests and see the patient first before I allow anyone in."

If everything's under control, Olivia wondered, then why no visitors? *She* was the person most concerned here. How long was she going to have to wait to find out what was wrong?

CHAPTER

21

Olivia was relieved to see Dr. Graham come into the room, carrying a file full of papers and a few developed X rays. It felt like she'd been waiting for hours.

"One thing I can tell you right away," said Dr. Graham, "is that there's nothing wrong with your heart."

"But what about this pain I've had?" Olivia protested.

Dr. Graham listened as Olivia described the pain again, then shrugged. "Most likely a pulled muscle. And probably some cartilage inflammation. It's not uncommon."

It seemed almost too good to be true. "But how does that explain the other things I've been feeling? My heart pounding the way it has . . . those flushed feelings. . . ."

"It won't," Dr. Graham agreed. "That's what

we're going to talk about now. To see if we can figure out this mystery together."

Dr. Graham asked Olivia to describe her symptoms and when they occurred, and to tell her a bit about what she'd been doing lately.

After listening for a while, the doctor held up her hand. "You probably know that I've already spoken with your boyfriend and your parents. From what you all say, I'd conclude that your symptoms are psychosomatic."

"But that can't be! I really felt those things! I didn't just make them up."

"Of course," Dr. Graham assured her. "They were real symptoms. I'm just saying that the cause had nothing to do with a physical illness."

"Then what — " Even as she asked, Olivia had more than an inkling of an answer. For one thing, she'd noticed as she was recapping her experiences for the doctor, that her worst bouts had all occurred after an unpleasant scene with her mother.

"Let me tell you a story that's kind of personal," Dr. Graham said.

"All the time I was studying to be a doctor, through college and medical school and even my internship, my mother did nothing but predict disaster. She was sure that I was going to catch some contagious germs from a patient, or ruin my eyes by studying. Or else ruin my whole life by concentrating too much on my career and not at all on socializing. She never once paid me a compliment.

"Then I finally got my appointment as a resident, and you know what?"

"What?"

"All of a sudden," answered Dr. Graham, smiling, "my mom became my biggest fan. All she could do was talk about 'my daughter, the doctor.' Even now, she practically drives her friends crazy with her bragging about me."

"But doesn't that make you mad?"

"It did a bit," Dr. Graham admitted. "But mostly I was surprised to see how quickly my mother grew up."

Olivia smiled. "I don't think mine will ever change," she said.

"Maybe not overnight. But as you grow up, you might find that your mom is growing, too. She's just scared on your behalf. Once she sees that you can handle the things you've undertaken, she won't have to be so afraid."

"I'm not doing too good a job of handling things lately, am I?" Olivia said glumly.

"I'm a little confused about that," Dr. Graham said. "From talking to Walt, it seems to me that on the one hand you're a little bit mad at your friends because they're graduating and leaving you behind. On the other hand you feel you owe it to them to uphold the honor of the group by doing well in cheerleading tryouts."

"That's their idea, not mine!" Olivia exclaimed.

"Is it? I doubt any of them cares about it as much as you do. None of them are all tied up in knots worrying about it the way you are."

"True," admitted Olivia. "But there's more. There's this whole thing about being captain next year if I make the squad at all. I feel I should want the honor, but I'm worried. I'm used to being the baby of the group, the one everyone looks out for — not the leader. I'm not sure I'd like being captain."

"Maybe you won't," said Dr. Graham evenly.

Olivia looked at her uncertainly. Then she brightened. "I think I get it," she said. "You're saying that it isn't that big a deal one way or the other."

"Exactly. You could always try it out. And if the role doesn't suit you, then give it up. The world will not end."

Olivia thought this over briefly. "I know you're right. It's too bad I couldn't have had this talk with you before I messed everything up."

"Oh, I don't think it's too late," Dr. Graham said. "It seems to me that it wouldn't hurt you to miss classes tomorrow morning and get some sleep. But I don't see any reason why you can't take part in this tryout. In fact, I prescribe it. And I plan to have a talk with your parents right now and explain my reasons."

Immediately after school the next afternoon, the hopefuls began gathering in the hall outside the gym where the tryouts were to be held.

Peter, Sally, and Betsey were among the first on the scene, and they huddled near the water fountain, exchanging last-minute advice and words of encouragement. Outwardly, Peter was his usual, collected self. Facing the judges didn't especially worry him, but he did keep casting longing glances in the direction of Hope Chang, who was looking even better than usual in her dramatic pink and black leotard and shocking-pink legwarmers.

Hope Chang hardly knows I exist, he thought to himself. At least not as someone who might mean something special to her. If we both do make the squad, though, there will be plenty of opportunity to get her to notice me.

For the time being, Hope's attention was riveted on Sean and Tara, who entered the hallway arm-in-arm. Tara was fairly bubbling, as if she and Sean shared some delightful and very private secret. Tara had arranged this entrance purposely, in the expectation of throwing Hope off balance. And at first, the tactic seemed to be more than working. Hope glared in Tara's direction, making Sean so uneasy that he eventually left Tara's side and stood by himself.

Tara made a beeline for Hope. "I tried to warn you about Sean," she said confidentially. "I hope you won't be too distracted thinking about him when it comes time to do your routine."

Hope lifted her chin in determination. "Not a bit. As a matter of fact, I plan to be thinking about you, Tara. You've done me a big favor. It takes a lot to get me angry, but anger usually does help me to do my best."

Tara's mouth dropped open. Her little plan to bother Hope had helped her to keep her mind off her own nervousness. Now, at the last minute, she felt suddenly terrified. She never had found a new outfit that she liked, so she was wearing the red leotard she'd used during practice. Privately, she felt sure that the judges would notice this and hold it against her. Other girls might get away with wearing the same clothes, but Tara Armstrong was expected to be a fashion plate. That was part of her image.

A short way down the hall, Rob Reynolds was seated on a bench in front of his locker, trying to concentrate his energy for the test ahead.

Rob had recovered from his sprained ankle in time to resume practice. But it still pained him from time to time, and he hoped that he wouldn't be too tentative when it came to jumping on it.

Rob was massaging the tricky ankle one last time when Samantha Gray floated his way and sat down beside him. Dressed in a powder blue warm-up suit, Samantha looked serene and slightly above it all, as usual. They hadn't spoken since their disastrous date.

"I guess I overdid it with some of those things I said to you on that hike," Samantha said apologetically. "I know now that I should have worn old clothes. So it wasn't all your fault that I ruined my sweater."

"Your sweater!" Rob was incredulous. "What about my ankle? Hasn't it occurred to you that it was partly your fault I sprained it?"

Samantha looked so taken aback, that it occurred to Rob that Samantha really hadn't connected his sore ankle with their fall on the hiking trail until this very moment.

"Then I guess it is up to me to be sorry," she said in a voice so low that Rob could hardly hear her.

As Samantha floated away again, Rob shook his head in confusion. Samantha was so pretty, but he had less of an idea than ever of what was going on inside her head.

Angie Poletti was headed toward the gym, coming from her last-period class, when she ran into Carla. "Good luck," she said, giving Carla a pat on the shoulder. "You've improved so much these last few weeks and worked so hard, I know you have a good chance."

"Forget the work," said Carla anxiously. "How do I look? Can you tell that I've lost just tons of weight?"

"Oh sure. You look a lot thinner," lied Angie. Now that Carla mentioned the subject, she could see a difference, but there had been no magical transformation.

Carla seemed to think that she looked like a different person, even if it wasn't strictly true. "I've been practically fasting all week. I plan to knock 'em dead," she said feistily.

By the time Angie reached the door to the gym, Pres and Nancy and Mary Ellen were there waiting for her. They stood together watching the latecomers.

Jessica arrived with her two older brothers along for moral support. She looked a shade or two paler than usual. She's scared, Angie thought. I wouldn't have expected that.

Holly Hudson, on the other hand, was the picture of confidence. "It's too bad about Olivia," Holly said to the seniors as she sailed by. "But I guess no one is too surprised that she stayed away from school today. The whole world could see that she wasn't up to facing the competition."

"Don't celebrate quite yet," snapped Mary Ellen. "Olivia is coming. She'll be here any minute."

Holly shrugged and went on inside, while the seniors stared at each other uneasily. They had all heard from Walt that Olivia was all right and planning to attend the tryouts, but none of them was quite sure what shape she would be in.

They got their answer shortly when Olivia showed up, with Walt at her side.

"Are you sure you're feeling all right?" Angie asked immediately. "We talked it over and we wanted you to know that if you aren't up to this, it's okay. You don't owe us anything."

"Thanks, gang, but I'm in the running." Olivia told them. "And believe it or not, I'm only moderately terrified."

The tryouts began with all the candidates lining up on the gym floor together, running through a repertoire of basic cheers.

This year, however, the judges had decided to make the second part of the audition private. Since it didn't seem quite fair to them that some people had friends and supporters present while others didn't, no audience was allowed. Everyone, even the senior squad, had to wait out in the hall while the judges called in the candidates one by one, to perform their special routines.

"I don't think this system is fair to us. I can't stand not knowing," Mary Ellen complained as they stood around watching the candidates emerge from the gym, trying to guess from the way they looked how things had gone.

A few hopefuls, their ordeal over, were ready and willing to rate their own efforts.

Holly Hudson emerged grinning broadly and flashed a "V for Victory" sign. She summed up her performance in one word: "Perfect!"

"Do you believe it?" Pres asked the others.

"Not really," said Mary Ellen. "But then again, it might have been good enough."

Carla, on the other hand, was more candid. "I would have done better if I hadn't practically fainted in the middle of my routine. So much for fasting. I think I'll go drown my sorrows in chocolate ice cream."

Most of the others, though, came out smiling more or less nervously, but without any firm predictions one way or the other.

Olivia was the last to be called in, and she was one of the few to emerge from the gym with no doubts about how she had done. "I'm definitely in," she announced as she rejoined the others. "They told me right away. The others are going to find out the results later this afternoon," she added, "but I'm not planning to wait around. I'm going to go call Dr. Graham and tell her thanks."

CHAPTER

At dawn, a big salmon-colored sun rose over the far end of the lake, turning the low-lying mantle of clouds a blush-pink. Field Day had arrived.

At the Kirkwood house, Mary Ellen's little sister Gemma got up first and ran over to the window of the bedroom she shared with Mary Ellen, to check the weather. "Oh-oh," she recited, "Red sky at morning, sailors take warning."

Mary Ellen turned over in bed and opened one eye. "Go back to sleep, Gemma. It's too early to get up."

"But it's going to rain today. The weatherman predicted it. And so does the saying we learned in school."

"It is *not* going to rain," Mary Ellen said sleepily. "I promise you."

"Come on, how do you know?"

"Not after all we've been through. I just know

that it wouldn't dare rain on the day we get to wear our uniforms for the last time."

Mary Ellen was right.

By nine o'clock the cloud cover had mostly burned off and the sun was shining through. The warm spell was over and it was going to be a clear, but cool, day. Mary Ellen thought this might not be such a bad thing. It meant that the squad would be able to appear wearing the letter sweaters that they used all year and loved so much, instead of the white skirts that they wore only a few times during the warmer part of the year.

By the time Mrs. Kirkwood dropped Gemma and Mary Ellen off at the school, the area around the building was already bustling with activity. In the early afternoon the Tarenton High Marching Band would put on a show in the stadium, followed by the introduction of next year's cheerleading squad — the high point of the day. Mr. and Mrs. Kirkwood, along with most of the other parents, would be turning out to join the audience for that.

In the meantime, there was a full schedule of Field Day competitions and activities, along with a fair, with booths organized by various community groups and craftspeople. Most of the booth sponsors had been on the scene and hard at work for hours, setting up their wares and getting ready for business.

Gemma ran off almost immediately, to take part in some foot races for younger children that were being held on the track in the football stadium. Mary Ellen, who'd arrived in street clothes — shorts and a light sweater — headed for the locker room under the stadium to stash her uniform.

Angie was already in the locker room, hanging up her neatly pressed and pleated cheerleading skirt.

"I almost can't believe it," Mary Ellen said wistfully as she opened her locker and set about unpacking her own things. "We'll never have the right to wear these colors again. Not as official Tarenton High Cheerleaders. I wonder what we'll all be doing a year from now at this time."

Angie laughed ruefully. "I'll probably be doing pretty much the same thing I'm doing now, in a way. Cramming for final exams and wondering how I can possibly pass them."

Mary Ellen shot her a look of surprise. "Does that mean that you finally decided to go to State? What happened to your idea of staying around to help your mother in the beauty shop?"

"Mom vetoed that one," Angie explained. "I might have kept trying to change her mind, except that Chris agreed with her. So I was outvoted."

"And you accepted that?"

"Chris pointed out that my real talent wasn't for making people look good on the outside, but for making them feel good on the inside. I guess he convinced me. So I've decided to major in social work at State."

"I'm happy for you Angie." Mary Ellen hugged her. "I agree with your mom and Chris. I think you'll be a terrific social worker."

"I'll second that," said Nancy Goldstein, who had just arrived in the locker room. "By the way, I've made my plans, too. I sent off my acceptance to Brown this morning. I just wish I could say that Eric was as happy about my decision as Chris is about yours.

"We didn't exactly break up," Nancy went on, "but Eric would have liked me to stay closer to home. The thing is, as much as I care for him, I just knew that wouldn't be right for me. My motto is, 'Go East, young woman.'"

Just then, Coach Engborg came in, staggering under an armload of uniforms for the new squad, swathed in plastic bags. "We narrowly avoided a last-minute crisis," she told them. "These just arrived. At least we won't have to worry about having a tailor adjust them until later."

Mary Ellen helped Ardith hang the girls' uniforms on hooks at one end of the dressing room, and Ardith departed to find someone who would deliver the boys' outfits.

"There they are," said Mary Ellen, pointing to the neat row of brand-new uniforms. "Our replacements waiting to make us seniors obsolete. I wonder if there really *is* life after cheerleading."

"Of course there is," giggled Nancy and Angie in unison.

Mary Ellen nodded, but she wasn't quite as sure as the others. Out of the entire squad, she was the one who had supposedly known exactly what she wanted with her future. She was the ambitious one, headed for New York and an exciting career in modeling, possibly even in acting.

Now everyone else seemed to have worked out

definite plans, and she was still feeling twinges of doubt.

Mary Ellen followed the other girls outside where they found Patrick waiting for them.

"Great news, ladies," he announced. "A new event has been organized at the last minute — a relay race for couples. There will be three couples from each class, and participants in varsity sports aren't eligible. So I took the liberty of organizing the senior contribution to the fun."

"Some liberty!" Mary Ellen grasped. "And now I suppose you're going to tell us that we're competing, thanks to your bright idea."

"Exactly." Patrick beamed with pride in his own initiative. "Angie and Chris are one couple — Chris has already said he'd do it. And, of course, you and I will run together, Mary Ellen."

"And if we don't want to?"

"You have no choice," Patrick said happily. "It's for fun. It's for charity. And besides, how would it look if you senior squad members chickened out once you've already signed up?"

"Well, at least I'm out of this," said Nancy with relief. "Since Eric isn't a student."

"Not quite. I have a partner picked out for you, Nancy. Mr. Preston Tilford III himself."

Nancy looked doubtful. "Can Pres run? I don't think he's used his legs as a means of transportation since the day he got his driver's license."

"Oh, Pres can run very fast when he wants to," Patrick assured them.

The girls laughed. "We all know that," Nancy teased. "And by the way, where is Pres? And Walt? And Livvy?"

"I'll show you," said Patrick. "You'd never believe it if I told you."

He led them back to the hillside behind the stadium where most of the booths were located. Olivia met them, explaining that she'd been drafted into running a student-council booth to raise money for the Debating Club's travel fund.

She pointed to a booth that was located on the flat area at the base of the hill. A good-sized, above-ground pool had been set up and filled with water. Suspended over it were three swing-type seats, each with a large painted target above it. "The object is to throw rubber balls at the target. If you get a direct hit, the seat collapses and the guy in it gets dunked."

The three seats were occupied at the moment by Walt, Pres, and Sean Dubrow. All of them looked a bit chilly, but good-humored as they fended off occasional badly aimed balls and dared the customers to dunk them.

"We're doing a fantastic business," Olivia said, "Especially with the girls. Of course, Vanessa is our best customer."

Vanessa had been front and center among the booth's customers, and as Olivia spoke she got off a lucky throw that hit the target above Pres, sending him splashing into the water. He emerged from the pool sopping wet, but still grinning.

A few minutes later Pres was replaced by another male volunteer, and he wrapped himself in a blanket and joined the group. "I never thought I'd enjoy being a target for Vanessa Barlow," Pres said, "but it's all for a good cause. Besides, she needs this today. I don't think I've ever seen her so steamed."

Olivia filled them all in. It seemed that Vanessa's grades were not quite up to college standards. So her father, Dr. Barlow, the Tarenton superintendent of schools, had talked her into spending a year at a very fancy academy in Switzerland.

"Switzerland!" said Mary Ellen. "Some people have all the luck!"

"That's what Vanessa thought," Pres put in. "Only after she said yes and her dad paid the bill she found out that the place is a sort of finishing school for females only. And very strict, too. I hear that they expect students to get up at six-thirty in the morning and clean their own rooms before breakfast."

"And that," said Nancy, "is sure to finish Vanessa."

Pres went off to shower and change, and the others gravitated towards the practice field where the relay race was to be held. Hank Vreewright, the lanky basketball player, was acting as judge, and he explained the rules. The boys would run the first lap, once around the quarter-mile track, and then pass their batons to the girls, who would complete the second lap.

"Ugh," groaned Mary Ellen. "How do I let Patrick get me into these things?"

Angie, meanwhile, was looking over the competition. In addition to three sophomore couples, the runners were Betsey, paired with Peter Rayman; Jessica and a boy named Terry Hunt; and

— to her surprise — Carla and her own brother Andrew.

"I think I'm starting to take this race seriously," she said. "I'm not quite ready to let my younger brother get the better of me."

Pres arrived fashionably late as usual, taking his place at the starting line seconds before the gun was fired. He made a quick getaway, though, and to everyone's amazement, soon took the lead in the field of nine.

"Way to go!" cheered Nancy. "Come on!"

"Who would have thought?" Mary Ellen said.

Pres was still ahead as he passed the baton to Nancy at the end of his lap. Chris, Peter Rayman, and Andrew were close behind, along with one of the sophomores. Patrick, who was muscular but not speedy, was running dead last.

Nancy did her best, but couldn't hold the lead Pres had established. Angie Poletti and Carla both passed her on the backstretch and were running side-by-side as they entered the last straightaway.

"Push it, girl," Angie muttered to herself as fought to maintain her stride. All those morning runs she'd started doing just to keep in shape were coming to her aid now. If only she could make the finish line. . . .

With a few yards to go, Angie found a new reservoir of speed and pumped her legs in a sprint for the finish. She broke the hand-held tape just inches ahead of Carla.

The rest of the cheerleaders were ecstatic. "See that," huffed Pres, still catching his own

209

breath. "That victory ought to prove that we're not obsolete yet."

Still, the inevitable moment could not be delayed.

Less than an hour later, the Tarenton High Marching Band took to the field in full regalia, filing onto the field to the music of "Stars and Stripes Forever."

Mary Ellen and the other cheerleaders, in uniform now, waited patiently on the ramp leading to the locker rooms while the band put on its show. Then they ran onto the field and took their places for the playing of the alma mater.

Now, for the last time, it was the old squad's turn to do its thing.

Mary Ellen raised her megaphone. "Tarenton Tri-umph!" she yelled.

"That's what it will be," the crowd responded.

"Tarenton *tri*-umph!
VIC–TOR–Y!"

They did the "Growl Wolves, Growl" cheer, and the fight song, and then a routine that was a shortened version of the break dance pregame show that Walt had developed.

Mary Ellen had never enjoyed the dancing part of the routine as much as she did this day. She drank in the music and the cheers of the crowd, wishing that the moment could go on forever.

As a finale, the squad formed a pyramid, with

smiling Olivia alone on the top. The crowd roared its approval.

Then they dissolved the pyramid, Olivia making the descent from her perch look easy. The squad formed a line facing the spectators and Mary Ellen stepped forward to take the microphone that Ardith held out to her.

"As this year's captain," she said, "it gives me great pleasure to announce the members of the junior class who will be taking our place as your new cheerleaders in the year to come. As I call out their names and they join us on the field, please give them each a big hand. We ask that, before lining up on the field, each new cheerleader take a pompon from one of the old cheerleaders."

Mary Ellen paused to take a deep breath. Then she began.

"Sean Dubrow."

Sean bounded out of the stands, waving his arms excitedly. He accepted Nancy's pompon with a wink. He'd known he'd make the squad all along.

"Peter Rayman."

Peter, seated beside Sally and Betsey, didn't seem to hear Mary Ellen's announcement. But the girls shook him excitedly and pushed him up off the hard bench. Peter made his way to where Sean was standing and took Angie's pompon with a shy smile.

"Jessica Bennett."

Jessica gave a cry of relief and delight. After she took a pompon from Walt and turned to face the crowd, she knew she was in her element. She could barely contain her excitement.

"Hope Chang."

Hope had been sitting off to one side of the stands, nervously clenching and unclenching her fists. When she heard her name she wasn't sure she could stand, much less take her place on the field in front of all those people. But the next thing she knew Pres was putting a pompon into her hand and she was in line next to Jessica. So *this* was cheerleading.

"Tara Armstrong."

Beaming, Tara stepped out on to the field. She'd made it, and she meant to enjoy every minute of being a cheerleader. She accepted a pompon from Mary Ellen and held it high in the air.

Everyone waited expectantly for Mary Ellen's final anouncement. Peter and Sean exchanged a brief handshake. They had gotten along well enough in practice, but there was already a sense of rivalry between them.

Jessica Bennett glowed with happiness. She'd been ecstatic ever since she'd heard her name called, and she was still so excited that she did a spontaneous series of cartwheels on the field, earning an extra cheer from the crowd.

The broad smile that was plastered on Hope Chang's face looked convincing from the viewpoint of the stands. But the new squad members standing next to her could tell that it was just a mask to cover her nervousness. Hope had worked hard for her victory, barely taking the time to imagine what it would be like if she actually won. Only now was she starting to wonder whether she was going to enjoy the fruits of her success.

Would she *ever* fit in with this group? She wasn't at all sure.

Tara was barely conscious of the other new cheerleaders standing beside her. Tara's entire attention was focused on the response from the stands. She was a natural actress and leader, qualities that the judges had recognized that separated her from several other promising candidates — including Holly, who had tried too hard; and Samantha Gray, who had seemed completely self-absorbed.

Tara, however, hadn't a clue as to what the judges had seen in her. She assumed that she had won on the basis of extra points for her appearance. As long as she was on the field, that didn't worry her. But she wasn't at all sure that she would be able to last through a whole year of practices and activities. Sooner or later, Coach Engborg would discover the insecure Tara hiding inside her flashy exterior. The other cheerleaders would discover it, too. Winning had made her feel like more of a fake than ever.

Finally, Mary Ellen continued.

"And last, but by no means least," Mary Ellen said slowly, "Tarenton High's new cheerleading captain, Olivia Evans."

Olivia had never looked prettier or more confident, as she took the microphone from Mary Ellen, and led the crowd in a locomotive cheer, her first as captain.

"Well, it's all over," said Nancy to Angie, as they filed off the field behind the band.

"Except for Livvy," Angie pointed out. "Some-

213

how I can't help wondering how she's going to manage to co-exist on the same squad with Jessica Bennett. And for that matter, how Hope and Tara are going to manage to get along."

"And whether Peter Raymon will ever get Hope's attention," added Nancy.

"And who will finally end up with Sean Dubrow," concluded Angie.

Nancy sighed. "We're going to miss all the action. It's almost enough to make me regret that I'm graduating." She paused, then added, "Almost, but not quite."

CHAPTER

23

Mary Ellen was the last to leave the locker room. She changed slowly into her street clothes, hoping to have a chance to talk to Coach Engborg, to thank her for all her work and her faith in the squad. But the coach, busy giving instructions to the cheerleaders, didn't see Mary Ellen waiting around.

Of course, there'd be other chances to say goodbye to Coach Engborg, Mary Ellen told herself. But seeing the coach so completely wrapped up in dealing with the new squad was a jolting reminder that this stage of her life really was over.

Is there life after cheerleading?

She wasn't sure that the question was as silly as Angie and Nancy apparently thought it was.

Although it wasn't quite time to meet her family for the ride home, she couldn't stand to hang around the field house any longer. She wandered out to the parking lot where she found

215

Pres and Patrick busy looking over an old, rather battered delivery truck that had the words: SUN-SHINE BREAD in peeling paint on its side.

"How do you like my new wheels?" Pres asked proudly as Mary Ellen approached. "My folks bought this for me as a graduation present."

"You're kidding!" Mary Ellen studied Pres's expression, then Patrick's, before finally deciding that the two of them weren't pulling her leg.

"That was more or less my father's reaction," Pres said, grinning. "But I finally convinced him that I was serious about this moving business, so he gave in. This baby doesn't look like much, but we'll fix that. It has a new engine, though."

Pres patted the side of the van lovingly, then hopped into the driver's seat and chugged off for a test drive, leaving Mary Ellen alone with Patrick.

"Looks as if you definitely have a partner," Mary Ellen commented.

"For the business." Patrick shrugged. "But what I'd really like to have is a partner, you know, for life."

He took her hand and looked earnestly into her eyes. "I know this isn't much," he added. "Not compared to the kind of life you dream about. But it's real. And you could still be a part of it all, Mary Ellen, if you wanted to."

Mary Ellen had never found it easy to say no to Patrick. Just being close to him invariably made her feel weak in the knees. But this time, a little voice inside her head warned her that if she gave in, it would be for good. Patrick had joked about their getting married before. But this time he was completely serious.

The kind of life you dream about. . . .

Why did that phrase, out of everything Patrick had said, keep echoing in her mind?

"I'm sorry if I haven't always had very much sympathy for your plans for the business," she told him. "I can see now that this is the right future for you."

Patrick squeezed her hand harder.

Suddenly, though, Mary Ellen knew what she had to say. If only she could find the strength to make the words come out right.

"But the thing is, Patrick, it isn't *my* dream."

"What are you saying, Melon?"

"Just that I've got to at least try to make my own dream come true. The way you're trying with yours. Do you understand that? I've been thinking about leaving Tarenton, and becoming a big-name model since I was in junior high school. I've got to at least make an effort to see if the fantasy can come true.

"I do love you," she went on. "But sooner or later, I'd look at you and wonder whether I'd made the right choice in giving up my dream. It wouldn't be fair to either of us."

Patrick's hopeful expression had deflated into a frown. His eyes, so sparkling a few seconds ago, were misted over with tears. "You're serious, aren't you?" he said.

"I'm afraid so."

"Okay." He kissed her lightly on the forehead. "I do understand, believe it or not. But I can't

217

help hoping. Maybe after you've tried New York for a year or so, you'll see that what Tarenton has to offer — what I have to offer — is the best dream after all."

"Maybe," she said.

After that, it seemed that they had run out of things to say to each other. They stood arm-in-arm until Pres brought the truck back, exclaiming over its smooth ride. Then Patrick climbed into the passenger side of the cab, and drove off with Pres.

As the van pulled away, Mary Ellen could see Patrick's face, looking back at her with a mixture of hurt and hopefulness.

Maybe, she thought. Maybe Patrick's faith would win out after all, and a year from now she'd be answering the same question from him in a different way. Who could tell? But deep down inside, she had a feeling that a chapter in her life had ended once and for all.

Hearing laughter and shouting, Mary Ellen turned and saw the new squad, all but Olivia, coming into the parking lot. They were obviously unable to contain their joy, their good feelings, their excitement. They were kissing each others' cheeks, and wrapping their arms around each other, running, hopping, jumping. Their laughter was loud and free.

They stopped when they saw Mary Ellen watching them. Her heart was full of many things: envy, because she knew how exciting the year ahead of them was; happiness for them because they had made the squad; and enthusiasm

and concern for her own coming year. She smiled
at them and shouted, "Good luck!"

The new squad members were whispering
among themselves. Then they separated. They
formed a straight line, hands on their hips, feet
set apart. They raised their arms and yelled:

"Give me an M . . . M!
Give me an A . . . A!
Give me an R . . . R!
Give me a Y . . . Y!
Give me an E . . . E!
Give me an L . . . L!
Give me an L . . . L!
Give me an E . . . E!
Give me an N . . . N!
MARY ELLEN, MARY ELLEN!
RAH–RAH–RAH!"

An exciting excerpt from Pulling Together, *Cheerleaders #21, follows:*

Cheerleaders #21
PULLING TOGETHER

When the telephone rang, Jessica Bennett grabbed for it as if she were trapped in a burning building and the telephone was a ladder to safety. Thankfully, its shrill ring had interrupted yet another "discussion" with her mother Abby and her stepfather Daniel — yet another "discussion" about the same old thing. . . .

"Jessica?" the telephone voice said. "This is Ardith Engborg."

Jessica's green eyes brightened. Mrs. Engborg was the tiny, blonde Tarenton High School cheerleading coach. Shivering happily, Mrs. Bennett's only daughter let the knowledge that she was now a Varsity Cheerleader temporarily brush aside the unpleasantness of the argument. Ever since shortly after tryouts last spring, her wonderful uniform — a red wool skirt with white pleats, a heavy white sweater with a big red "T" on the front, and white tennis shoes — had been waiting in her closet for practice to begin. Often throughout the summer she'd slip into the outfit and do some practicing on her own, until Daniel would shout for her to "Quit all that jumping around up there before the ceiling falls in on us!"

"Jessica, I'm planning some concentrated practice for next week. I've borrowed a cabin out at the lake. School begins the week after next and since all of you except Olivia are new, we have our work cut out for us. We'll meet at the school Monday morning at eight o'clock and go on from there."

Jessica realized she wasn't being presented with an invitation as much as she was being given an order. It was put very nicely, but it was still obviously a command. Mrs. Engborg hadn't even asked her if she could make it.

But of course she could. Anything to get out of this zoo! In geometry class she had always hated triangles, and now she knew why. It had been so much better with just her and her mother after her two older brothers had grown up and left home. Then Daniel came along. And if he hadn't exactly ruined everything, he sure had put a big dent in her life.

She was happy her mother had someone, after being alone for so long. Jessica's father had died when his daughter was just ten years old. And Daniel tried, he really did. But Daniel in the family was like an elephant in a ballet. He just didn't know how to fit in.

"What should I bring?" she asked Ardith.

"Plenty of exercise gear, a sleeping bag, flashlight, toothbrush . . ." the coach rattled off. "No radios, please. We'll have the tape machine for music. And you may bring swimming things. You'll have a little time off to unwind." She laughed. "Kindly remember that word *little*."

"Yes, ma'am." Who was she to argue? A whole week out of the house — perfect! She couldn't wait!

"Monday morning, eight o'clock," Ardith said. "See you then," she added, and hung up.

Jessica didn't feel like resuming the argument now. But her stepfather had no way of knowing that one brief phone call had drastically changed her mood.

"Abby, I just don't understand," he jumped right in, "why you bought her another sweater. Her closet already looks like a department store."

Abby, her pretty face flushed, gently laid a hand on her tall, thin husband's arm. "C'mon, Dan," she said softly, "you're exaggerating. Besides," she added, glancing nervously toward Jessica, who leaned against the refrigerator holding the offending pink sweater in her hands, "now that Jessica is a cheerleader, she needs a few nice things. She's representing her school."

Unimpressed, Daniel replied, "She's also representing this family. And this family has bills."

Jessica thought to herself, I know what's coming now. With Daniel's back to her, she silently mouthed toward her mother: Considering the small fortune that uniform cost. . . .

"Considering the small fortune that uniform cost," Daniel grumbled, turning to face both of them and catching Jessica in the act, "she should wear nothing but that for the next twenty years!"

Grateful that he had apparently chosen to ignore her mimicry and anxious to escape, Jessica said sweetly, "I'm sorry I'm such a financial drag, Daniel. I've some money saved from baby-sitting. I'll give it to Mom for the sweater, okay?" Turning to her mother, she held up the sweater and said, "Thanks, Mom. It's really gorgeous!"

Silent at last, Daniel busied himself making a ham sandwich at the counter. Jessica told them about Ardith's phone call, adding quickly, before her stepfather could say anything, "And it won't cost a cent. I already have all the stuff I need."

Was that relief she saw in her mother's eyes, green like her own, at the thought of Jessica being gone for a whole week?

Well, why not? Who could blame her? Life in the Bennett household wasn't exactly terrific these days. Jessica tried to tell herself that it couldn't be just *her* fault, but sometimes it was really hard. With her brothers, Gary and John, grown and hardly ever around, any family trouble almost always revolved around Jessica. After all, her mother and Daniel loved each other. It was hard to ignore the obvious fact that without Jessica around, they'd be just fine.

Well, they'd have a whole week of peace while she was at the lake. And after that, she'd be so busy with school and cheerleading, she'd just be dashing in and out of the house. That should help.

It had to help. It just *had* to!

Excusing herself, she left the kitchen and went to her room to check out her swimming suits. Should she take the bikini or the one-piece — or both? Major decision, she thought, grinning happily as she closed her bedroom door.

Sean Dubrow wasn't home when his cheerleading coach called. But he checked the answering machine the minute he walked in the door. Most of the recorded messages were for his father, which came as no surprise to Sean. Mark Dubrow, Tarenton Fabricators' top salesman, played as hard as he worked. The tall, good-looking widower had many friends.

But Sean wasn't exactly a loner, and he had his share of recorded calls, too. The only one that caught and held his attention was the one from Ardith Engborg. Flopping down on the long, dark leather couch, his sneakered feet resting on the metal-studded arm, he replayed his coach's message.

"Well, all *right*!" he shouted into the big, empty living room when he had replaced the receiver. "A week at the lake! What a way to cap off the summer!"

Still lying on the couch, his mind zipped down the list of girls who would be sharing that week with him: Olivia Evans, tiny, pretty, brownish hair, the only veteran on the squad. A great gymnast. He'd always gotten a big kick out of watching Olivia's small, compact body fly through the air in the gym or on the football field, light as a plastic Frisbee.

But Olivia was Walt Manners' girl friend and had been, practically forever. Of course, Sean reflected, staring up at the beamed ceiling, Walt graduated last June and wouldn't be returning to the squad. So . . . who knew? Maybe little Olivia would be lonesome without Walt.

That Tara Armstrong. She was like the cover of some fashion magazine — long red hair and with a body that was perfect. Having something going with Tara would be handy, too, because she lived in his neighborhood, in a big English Tudor house a couple of blocks away. And word around school was that Tara was always looking for fun. Maybe it was that hair. How could anyone with hair that looked like fire be dull?

"Hey, hey, hey!" Mark Dubrow sang out as he slammed shut the front door. "Anybody home?"

"In here!" Sean called. It was nice, just the two of them rattling around in this big house, no one nagging at them or telling them to keep their feet off the couch or coffee table. Not that his mother had been like that. She hadn't. But a couple of the housekeepers his dad had hired had driven both of them crazy. Nag, nag, nag!

"Whew, what a day!" his father said, yanking loose his tie and collapsing into a chair. His tweed sportcoat boasted suede elbow patches. Sean thought the jacket made both of them look intellectual, and he borrowed it whenever he wanted to impress a female member of the honor society. His father wore it when *he* wanted to impress a female faculty member at the Hillsborough Junior College.

"Windy leave us any food?" his father asked, his eyes closed.

"Windy" was their nickname for Mrs. Natalie Windsor, the middle-aged woman who came in every day to tidy up and fix their evening meal. They seldom saw her and seldom ate the meals she cooked, more often eating out. But without her "tidying up," Sean knew, the place would, within twenty-four hours, look as if it had been bombed. It had always amazed him that his father could go out of the house looking so put-together, yet his room was a real disaster, just like a little kid's room. Just like Sean's room.

"Yeah. Some chicken stuff. Smells great." His dad looked really beat. Maybe Sean would stay home tonight. They could rent a movie for the VCR.

"Sound good?" Sean asked, following his suggestion that they do just that.

"Yeah, sure, sounds great. But no can do. Got a heavy date. You won't have any trouble polishing off that casserole a lá chicken, will you? A growing 'hunk,' as your countless girl friends probably refer to you, needs plenty of fuel."

Sean grinned. "Look who's talking about countless girl friends! Who had most of the messages on the recorder?"

"Those weren't girls. Those were women. There's a difference, my friend, believe me. Listen Sean, between work and play, I'm gonna be running on all six cylinders this week, okay? I've got a schedule that would give a weaker man a stroke." He grinned wearily. "You be okay here without your old man? Windy'll feed your face, okay?"

Sean didn't expect to be home to eat any of Windy's food, and told his father so. "No sweat. Cheerleading coach called. The squad is spending all week at the lake. Have to get in shape for when we go out on the field to stun and dazzle the audience, right?"

"Hmmm?" Mark Dubrow looked up, opening his eyes. "Oh, sure. Well, good, we're all set then. Now I have to hit the showers, kid. See you later. Okay if I borrow your navy tie? The knit one?"

"Oh. Sure. I won't be needing a tie out at the lake."

When his father had gone, Sean returned to the business of picking a Varsity Cheerleader to zero in on. But somewhere between Jessica (who might prove to be a real challenge) and Hope Chang (who was too quiet), he fell asleep and dreamed about how quickly, now that he was a cheerleader, his own little black book would make his father's look like the tiniest of pamphlets.

Hope Chang sighed as she hung up the powder-blue Princess phone on her bedside table. It was time. She'd known it was coming. My life as a Varsity Cheerleader, she thought grimly, is about to begin. I should keep a journal and write a book about it someday. Her stomach felt like it had a hole in it. A whole week with people she didn't know well, people who weren't anything like her, doing something she wasn't even sure she really wanted to do. Would the week be a disaster?

She had never expected to be picked as a Varsity Cheerleader. Trying out had been her mother's idea. It was hard to say no to her mother. Or her father, for that matter. Caroline and Henry Chang simply took for granted obedience from their children. And so far, Hope and her little brother James hadn't disappointed their parents.

Why, Hope wondered resentfully, hadn't it been enough that she was an A student, played both the violin and the piano well enough to be first soloist at the Music Academy's recitals, had read many of the classics, and was her homeroom representative on the student council last year? Why couldn't her parents have been satisfied with that?

Chosen or not, she didn't *feel* like a Varsity Cheerleader. Would an entire week with five others who did feel like members of the squad make *her* feel like one, too?

She didn't want to go. But she would. Because she was expected to go. And Hope Elizabeth Chang always did what was expected of her.

Always.

Olivia Evans, who was sitting cross-legged on her bed planning for the week at the lake, was *very* worried about the competition heading her way.

Tara was so gorgeous, and Hope was a real darling, so sweet and pretty and anxious to do the right thing. But it was Jessica Bennett who really worried her. On the old squad, Olivia had never felt quite as nice as Angie Poletti, quite as smart as Nancy Goldstein, or anywhere near as pretty as Mary Ellen Kirkwood, their captain. But she'd always known her years of gymnastic training had given her her own special something.

Now here came Jessica Bennett, who sailed through the air as if she had wings, whose long, slender body seemed made of rubber, bending and curving in almost any direction with less effort than Olivia used to blink an eye.

Olivia had had "teamwork" hammered into her for so long, she felt as if it were tattooed on her chest. She knew how crucial it was to a unified squad. So she knew she shouldn't be thinking about Jessica, and she shouldn't be worried about the competition. She should be thinking of all of them as one single unit.

But she couldn't help it.

And maybe she wouldn't be quite as worried if Walt (her very *own* Walt) didn't look at Jessica as if he'd never seen a pretty girl before. His voice still said, "I love you, Olivia," but whenever Jessica was around, his dark brown eyes seemed to say, "On the other hand. . . ."

Olivia made a face and reached for an open bag of pretzels at her elbow. Taking one from the bag, she held it up in front of her and said aloud, "It's going to seem so strange, getting used to the new squad after spending so much time with Angie and Mary Ellen and Nancy and Pres. And Walt, of course. Why did they have to go and graduate, anyway?"

The pretzel stared back at her.

"Why couldn't at least *one* of them have flunked?" she asked it. "Then I wouldn't be all alone on this new squad."

Alone. As in "without Walt." How awful. Oh, he was still around and she'd seen a lot of him toward the end of the summer. But in another week, he'd be gone. Off to college. Without her. What would she do without him?

Both of the male cheerleaders were new this year. Sean Dubrow, she thought to herself, was gorgeous — with dark hair and eyes, and shoulders that could probably support the entire squad without effort. But he seemed so full of himself. Not her type.

Peter Rayman had sandy hair, a nice, lean face with high cheekbones, and eyes almost as blue as a clear October sky. But he was as different from warm, outgoing Walt as sugar is from salt. He'd be a hard person to get to know.

This week at the lake would give her a hint about how her senior year was going to go. It would give them all a chance to get to know each other.

Maybe, after a day or two, even Peter Rayman would relax.

Peter Rayman had a long way to go before he'd be able to relax about cheerleading. Ardith's telephone call had brought forth visions of seven straight days of Sean Dubrow. He shuddered, his slender but very solid frame shaking the wicker rocking chair. He hated wicker. It scratched his back and the backs of his thighs when he was wearing shorts. But his mom loved wicker, and had filled the apartment with it after the divorce.

He had barely replaced the receiver when his mother came into the room.

She had just come from her job at the hospital. She looked tired and hot, really exhausted. His mother was too smart to be just filing medical records, but it had been all she could find to do after being a housewife for so long. He knew the job bored her, but he also knew they had to eat. His dad wasn't all that great about sending them money.

There were bluish circles under her eyes. She didn't sleep much at night. Maybe it was the heat. He often heard her wandering around in the living room late at night. And he always wondered if it was her ex-husband keeping her awake . . . or worries about her son.

He just wished like crazy that she didn't take her responsibilities as a single parent so seriously. He was *okay*. Why couldn't she see that?

He didn't want to tell her about the phone call, but he had to.

"Oh, Peter, I just don't know," she said doubtfully when he had explained. She stood over him, her hands folded in front of her. "You're not going to be doing any waterskiing, are you?"

He flushed. Did she have to remind him that he wasn't the world's greatest swimmer? *One* little accident he'd had waterskiing, and she was going to remember it for the rest of her life!

And hadn't Sean Dubrow been on the swim team freshman year? Peter groaned silently.

"We're going to be practicing *cheers*, Mom. That's what it's all about."

She'd been happy about the cheerleading at first, thinking it sounded safe. Then she'd attended Field Day and had seen the human pyramid the retiring Varsity Squad had formed, and she'd been on his back ever since. He'd explained a thousand times that since he was strong and sturdy, he'd be on the *bottom* of any pyramid. But she went right on worrying about his falling from the top and "breaking every bone in your body."

"Peter, you stock up on suntan lotion. You know how easily you burn."

She made him feel like such a baby! He was much taller than her, but when she used that tone of voice, he felt so . . . small. It really didn't make him feel better to realize that she just couldn't help worrying all of the time. She cared.

And sometimes he really hated his father for leaving him there with her. She didn't know how to be a dad. She wasn't *supposed* to know how to be a dad. But to make up for it, she just did twice the mothering. It was driving him crazy.

Thank you, Mrs. Engborg, he thought gratefully as he went into the kitchen to fix scrambled eggs for their dinner. His mom would miss him next week, and she'd worry about him. He was sorry about that. But oh, he couldn't wait to get to the lake!

He even looked forward to competing with Dubrow.

Tara Armstrong's reaction to Ardith Engborg's telephone call was enormous relief, tinged with excitement. It had been such a long, boring summer. Those last few glorious days of school, when being a Varsity Cheerleader had actually become a reality for her, seemed so long ago. It had been impossible to hang onto that excitement through

mmer days. She had, even in her bore-
yed with the notion of getting a job.
on't be silly, darling," her mother had said
when Tara mentioned the idea. "At your age,
summer is for playing. Swimming, tennis, dating
— that's what summer is all about."

And when Tara mentioned that practically
everyone she knew had at least a part-time job,
her mother said lightly, "Well, then, isn't it lucky
that your daddy's a lawyer and brings home
enough money so that you don't *have* to work?"
Fluffing perfectly manicured nails through perfectly arranged blonde hair, she added, "Besides,
darling, what would you *do*?"

She had a point. It wasn't as if Tara was exactly
overloaded with experience. I can't type, she
thought, watching her mother set the card table
for her bridge party, and I haven't the slightest
idea how a word processor works. I don't even
know how to make a bed properly.

But then, why should she? That was what
Marie did. That's why Marie was their housekeeper — so that Tara and her mother had to do
very little.

When Tara mentioned the idea of working to
her father, he simply raised her allowance by another five dollars a week and went off to play
tennis at the country club. Joseph Armstrong
wasn't rich, but he was what Tara's mother called
"clever with money." They lived well.

The summer had dragged on like a bad movie.
Her mother had bridge and her father had tennis
and golf. Tara had cheerleading, but that was on

hold until fall. There were a few pa̲
everyone interesting seemed to have
from the face of the earth. She couldn't wa̲
school to start, to have her chance to be out the̲
on the football field in front of the whole school,
leading cheers. She had it in her to be a leader,
she was sure of that. Her grades weren't good
enough to make her the smartest in her class, and
she wasn't the most beautiful, although no one
had ever told her to put a bag over her head. But
she *could* be a leader on the squad, given half a
chance. At every game or pep rally she'd get to
wear that darling outfit, too. No one needed to
tell her it suited her. She had eyes, and she had
mirrors.

The week at the lake was exactly what she
needed. But more important, it was the beginning
of her time as a Varsity Cheerleader. A week was
more than enough time to size up the squad,
figure out which friendships were worth cultivat-
ing, and just exactly how she could become the
best cheerleader Tarenton had ever seen.

Moving gracefully across the room, curly red
hair trailing along her shoulders, Tara sat down
on the floor and dialed Samantha Gray's telephone number. They weren't exactly *best* friends,
but they *were* friends. Samantha had tried out
for cheerleading, too. Everyone had thought the
most popular girl in school was a cinch to make
the squad. And more than one of Samantha's
many friends had openly expressed their hostility and disappointment to Tara when she had
earned that honor instead. But Samantha had
seemed happy for her.

ell me this," Tara said when she had
d to Samantha about the week at the
Olivia and Jessica are both better gymnasts
an I am, so how am I going to keep from looking like a fool out there?" What she really wanted
to know was how she could manage to look better
than her squadmates, but Samantha wouldn't understand that.

"Olivia will help you," Samantha said with cer-
tainty. "She's an old hand at cheerleading, and
she's a nice person. I'm sure she'll give you lots
of tips."

Since Tara couldn't bear the thought of little
Olivia telling her what to do or how to do it,
she said nothing. But as she hung up, she couldn't
help wondering how Olivia Evans felt about the
new competition headed her way this fall.

JUNIOR HIGH

Coming soon from Scholastic — just in time for the back-to-school season — a brand-new series, JUNIOR HIGH!

Meet the latest crop of Cedar Groves Junior High eighth graders on their very first day of school. Join them in the chaotic cafeteria, the crowded corridors, the craziness of new classes. Get to know the students — from inseparable best friends Nora Ryan and Jennifer Mann, to the impossible class nerd, Jason Anthony; from rich and beautiful Denise Hendrix, to sports-maniac Mitch Pauley and sarcastic Susan Hillard. Share experiences with these eighth graders — the triumphs and setbacks, the friendships and first loves, the adjustments, the fun, and the occasional pain. Most of all, become a part of Cedar Groves Junior High, and the nonstop action that happens there.

Yo won't want to miss JUNIOR HIGH!, so watch for these titles:

Junior High Jitters (October 1986)

Class Crush (January 1987)

The Day the Eighth Grade Ran the School (March 1987)